AF260937

This book is a work of fiction. Names, places, events and characters are fictitious in every regard. Any similarity to actual events or persons, living or dead, is purely coincidental.

Bad-Ass Boys
Copyright©2014 Barry Lowe
ISBN 978-1-909934-84-9
Cover art and design by Dawné Dominique

Published by
Lydian Press 2014
Find us on the World Wide Web at
www.lydianpress.com

BAD-ASS BOYS
GAY MEN WHO CAN'T GET ENOUGH

Barry Lowe

Lydian Press

CONTENTS

All previously published as individual eBooks by Lydian Press

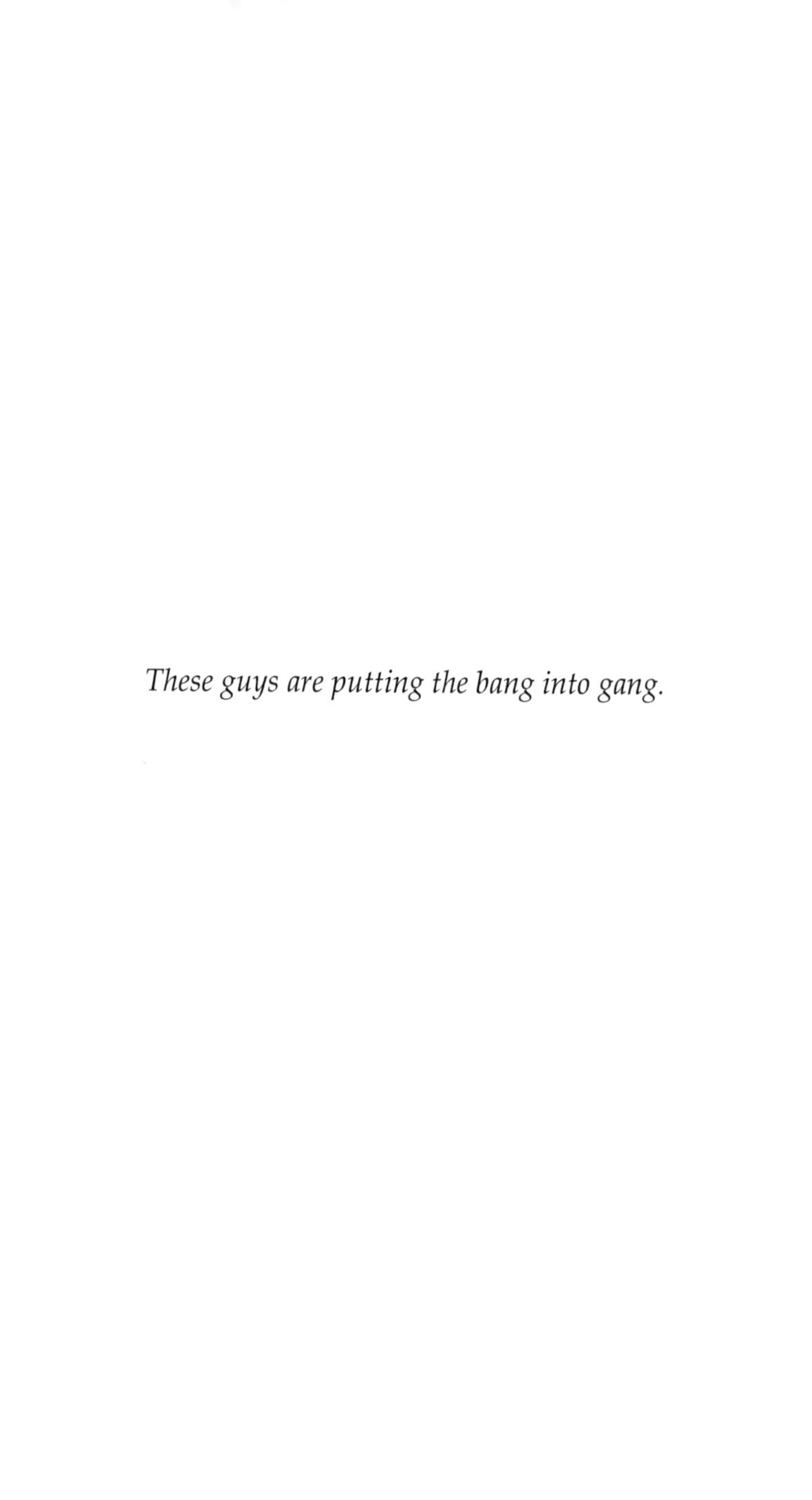

These guys are putting the bang into gang.

BREEDING MY BOYFRIEND

WTF? I awoke to the strains of some raucous pop tune getting louder and more insistent. It took my mind a moment or two to process I was at home, in my bed, and it was the middle of the night. Okay, that last item I wasn't totally sure of as yet as my eyes hadn't focused enough to read the blur of red figures on my digital clock. I grabbed my reading glasses, managing to put them up to my eyes. Not quite the middle of the night but one-thirty in the morning is close enough in my book.

The tune from Beyoncé or Björk or one of those divas with a squiggle above her name finally stopped before I could ascertain where the sound was coming from. Pop music was not part of my usual lifestyle at this hour of the morning unless my body was vertical in a crowd of likeminded semi-naked men at a club or a bar. As I was horizontal and I knew I hadn't been drinking or dancing or drugging, ergo I wasn't face down in a bar so I must be in bed.

A loud ping alerted me to the fact I had been correct in assuming the music was the ring tone on a mobile phone. The ping not only confirmed that and the fact the caller had left a message but also the whereabouts of said phone. I knew it wasn't mine because it lay on the bedside table as sleepy and unlit up as I wished I was. No, the sound came from under the bed.

Leaning over without actually getting out of bed, I hung upside down as I moved the covers aside to peer into the dark underbelly. Dangers lurked therein. Old tissues and a depleted tube of lube that had escaped our perfunctory once-a-week clean when we put on new sheets. We'd have to be more careful. We'd need rubber gloves before we could weed out all the sexual detritus that had accumulated.

Fortunately, the cell phone was hiding on the periphery, obviously having fallen out of Jesse's work trousers as he got ready earlier this evening. He'd be devastated without it – he lived on his phone. It was his contact with the outside world, his Sat Nav, his access to social media, it did just about everything except feed him, shelter him, and fuck him. I was responsible for all the above. I was the major breadwinner in our fourteen-month relationship, working nine-to-five-thirty in the well-paid corporate world while he went for auditions in the hope of becoming the next Ryan Kwanten of *True Blood* fame (whom he looked like) or, better still, the blond Tom

Cruise. He had the talent and the looks – all he needed was the breaks.

I didn't begrudge him that his meager wages from his job as an events waiter hardly added enough to pay for groceries each week. Plus, it was a pain that we had little chance to catch up with each other because he worked nights, usually until the early hours of the morning, and I worked days. All his best jobs were on the weekend. We were the proverbial ships in the night. I'd usually hear him return home and creep into bed when he kissed me softly on the cheek as he snuggled under the blankets smelling of soap and hair conditioner after washing off the stink of cigarettes and booze from the job.

In the mornings, it was my turn to kiss him on the forehead after brushing his blond locks aside. Normally, he'd grunt a greeting without really waking up. He'd sleep the morning away before getting up to have breakfast around noon, after which he'd head off to the gym or classes to keep his skills up. It was a hard life but he was determined to make it and I admired his grit and determination.

As I mentioned lube and tissues under the bed, we obviously did manage to occasionally indulge in sex. Usually on a Saturday or Sunday afternoon, although he didn't like anything too strenuous or exhausting because he had to work most weekend nights. Occasionally, he had a Sunday off. Or a couple of nights early in the week when all he wanted to do was slob in front of the telly. Or sleep. He seemed to need an awful lot of sleep.

He hated his waiter job, so he said, constantly groaning about the others not pulling their weight, or else Jack, the slimy boss putting the hard word on him to give up his ass. He knew if he charged him with sexual harassment he'd never work in the industry again. Not that the idea didn't appeal – to both of us – but we needed the little extra he brought in, especially the tips that paid for his extra-curricular acting activities, though why he needed to update his head shots every few months was beyond me. And the clothes. I had no idea where he managed to get so many well-made and fashionable items of menswear.

"You're such a snob, Costa," he admonished after I'd expressed surprise at his latest outfit. "Everyone knows that the big fashion houses dump their stock at charity stores after a showing or if they have too much stock. I have a friend, Claude, who runs one of the op shops and he gives me the heads up when the good stuff arrives. How else could I manage to look a million bucks otherwise?"

"I'm amazed they all seem to fit you to perfection," I groused.

"Oh, that. No, Claude is an absolute whizz with a sewing machine. A snip here, a tuck there, and voila!" He threw his arms in the air to show off not only the latest stunning menswear he had 'found' but also his svelte figure. He made me feel positively dowdy in comparison. He rushed to the mirror just inside the front door, tapping his chin with the upside of his hand. "Speaking of nip and tuck. I'm not sure how much longer I can put it off." He sighed theatrically.

I laughed which was the very worst thing to do.

He pouted. "Don't you want me to look my best for you? I'll never get any work if I have crow's feet and a sagging chin. What theatre directors are looking for is youth. Good looks. Why else do you think I have all those beauty products in the bathroom?"

That was a sore point between the two of us. His expensive toners and conditioners, wrinkle creams and eye drops, took up every spare inch of space so that my paltry items were crammed into the few nooks and crannies he left free.

"Jesse, you're twenty-three years old. You don't need all that gunk. Your skin is flawless. You're beautiful as you are."

"How do you think I retain my good looks, eh? By the judicial application of those very products, that's how."

We'd had this argument before. I maintained that the basics for good skin hydration was sorbolene and that he could buy it at the supermarket in five-gallon buckets cheaper than a single tube of one of his sorbolene-based products that also contained…

"It says here on the tube that it also has SHP+ and that's what makes the difference," he said proudly.

"What exactly is SHP+?" I asked.

He squinted but, without his glasses, he couldn't see a thing. "You're so bloody vain. Here, give it to me." Even I had difficulty reading the label where the asterisk explained the letters meant Super Hydrate Plus™. "It's made-up," I said in exasperation. "And merely adding a plus sign to something that already has plus in the description doesn't make it twice as good."

"Of course it does. They wouldn't be allowed to sell it if it wasn't genuine."

There was no arguing with Jesse when he was like this. Anyway, it wasn't coming out of the budget because, like the fashion wear, he had a source that supplied him with cut-price cosmetics. That only made them more dubious to my mind. Besides, he simply didn't need them. He was a magnificent looking specimen. I grant you, he probably looked better for his workouts at the gym, and I did so love his bubble butt and his abs and his…well, his whole body actually. I just wish he was less finicky when it came to me sticking my cock into it.

Jess has a phobia about germs. He won't let me eat his butt until he's showered and glistens like the Chrysler building in New York. I've tried to instigate spontaneous lovemaking by jumping him when he arrives home from work but he won't even kiss me or let me fondle his butthole until the obligatory shower. That rather takes the shine off it.

Still, I loved the bastard as much as I did when we first began dating. In fact, I loved him more and Jess confessed one night as I was plowing his hot ass that he was glad he met me and loved me more than life itself. Hyperbole, but it got the message across. Our mean-spirited friends said it would never last, that Jesse was too much the slut and I was too boring to keep such a magnificent animal satisfied and happy. High five to me. I had managed it. We were sublimely happy. Perhaps I could have been happier if Jess was available to me sexually on a more regular basis and if he'd just allow a little more spontaneity. I wouldn't mind as well if he'd swallow my junk every now and then – he spits it in a tissue – or if he took my load on his face or he actually managed to get my dick all the way into his mouth without putting his fist around it to stop me from poking his tonsils, or if he actually blew a load of his own before/during/or after I came. He tells me that my pleasure is everything and that he'll take care of himself later in the shower. He won't allow me to tug him off or suck him dry.

I love him. I really do.

I almost fell out of bed retrieving Jess's cell phone and I was about to place it on his night stand when I glanced at the screen. It was still illuminated and I noticed the message was from Sean. We didn't know a Sean. I knew all his contacts and suppliers by their first names but Sean had never been one of them. I even knew the names of his gym buddies. Perhaps Sean was an actor he'd recently befriended because he was always heading out to auditions for this small production or that indie short movie. Most of the short films he made sank without a trace, mainly because they were student projects for college. He was always promising to get some for his show reel but time was his enemy and he never got around to it or the student had left film school without a forwarding address. He could be slack like that sometimes. Surprising when he was so gung ho about his career normally.

Curiosity got the better of me. If Jess realized I'd read Sean's message and queried me I'd say I inadvertently hit the button as I was retrieving the phone. I didn't want him to think I was a snoop, although that's exactly what I was being. Who texts somebody at 1.30 in the morning? Unless it's important. An emergency maybe? Perhaps someone had been involved in an accident. Needed bail money. I'd tell him I thought it was important. That was my excuse.

The message was succinct. "gr8 2 meet u 2nite b over about 11 2 fuck yr tite ass." Obviously Sean was hot for the wrong ass. Jess and I are monogamous. It was the deal we struck right from the get go. Should I send him a message to tell him it was the wrong number? I didn't want Sean to turn up unexpectedly at eleven the next morning at our door while his 'tite ass' lover pined away at a different address. That wouldn't be fair.

I guess deep down I suspected Sean did, indeed, have the correct number. There was an easy way to find out. This time I didn't attempt to justify my spying. My sanity was at stake. My hands were trembling as I scrolled through messages from the past month, recognizing various names as his contacts for clothes, cosmetics, gym partners, with a few unfamiliar names sprinkled in between. I read the messages at random. 'yr hot give me a bell if u want a repeat hot ass.' 'titest hole evah want 2 fuk u all nite.' 'dump yr bf marry me.' They were all like that. I wanted to throw up. The bottom had fallen out of my guts.

Turning to his regulars, I tried Claude's most recent. If I hadn't already stumbled across Jess's double life, I may have read Claude's text as perfectly innocent. 'have a new load for u when can u cum 2 collect.' Did this mean Jess was swapping sexual favors for fashion? I tried Jules, his cosmetics supplier. 'got enuf cream here to cover yr fab face ring me.' One by one, his 'contacts' left highly suggestive messages: his portfolio photographer (head shot took on a whole new meaning); his personal trainer; his fellow thespians (male); his hairdresser. Plus a number of strangers whose texts suggested they'd just met Jess in the street or at one of the functions at which he was cater waitering.

I was exhausted just reading a few from the past month. I surmised some of these messages must be perfectly innocent otherwise Jess's ass would be shagged red raw. Oh, wait, hadn't he prohibited me from anal sex with him for ten days or more earlier because, so he said, he had hemorrhoids? I couldn't remember now whether that coincided with the period in which he'd received a myriad messages laced with so much innuendo I'm surprised his phone didn't orgasm.

Downstairs I poured myself a stiff drink because I'd even found a message from a guy at my office who'd glimpsed Jess when he turned up to meet me for dinner and a movie. Caz, one of the slimiest bastards you'd ever want to meet, wheedled Jess's number out of me by saying he was getting married and was looking for a waiter to serve at the reception. Mongrel. What he really wanted – obvious from his extremely explicit text – was a shot at Jess's butt. Caz had done everything to undermine me with the boss where we both worked. He was ambitious and I'd watched him stab quite a few fellow employees in the back in his relentless climb up the corporate ladder. My warning to Jesse about him must have paid off because he'd obviously rejected Caz's less-than-subtle advances.

Two vodka tonics later, numbness had set in, my heart anesthetized to the sheer volume of transgressions I'd read. Regardless, my mind wanted to hold on to the merest skerrick of doubt. I wanted to see for myself. First, I needed to ensure that it really was Jess's phone, although I knew it was because there were a few messages from me amongst the depravity, and, second, that the texts actually meant what I thought they did. If it was proof I was after where better to start than with Sean?

Although it was pitch black outside, I oiled the hinges on the kitchen door which led into the back yard, intending to leave it unlocked in the morning. It had a tendency to squeak loudly which I'm sure would act as an early warning system if I were to attempt to creep into the house to catch Jess unawares. I tested every door before turning my attention to the stairs to memorize which to avoid because they groaned under my weight. There were not many places to hide. The hall closet was ideal but there was no guarantee Jess wouldn't use it to hang his visitor's coat. None the less, I cleared out the rubbish so that I could use it if necessary. The kitchen's walk-in pantry was also an option after I'd moved boxes of goods that we'd stacked any old way through laziness, plus the fact I never expected to spend any time sequestered inside. There was also the closet in our bedroom. Dangerous, no doubt, although it was old-fashioned and had louvered shutters which opened for ventilation, wire mesh behind it to prevent moths and other creepy crawlies from getting into the clothes. It was too obvious except for the fact it was split in two and Jess had taken the larger side for himself, relegating me to the less commodious side. As far as I knew, he never looked in my section. That was ideal. Provided he used the bedroom for his assignation.

Not wanting to smell of booze, I cleaned my teeth and sucked a few peppermints before climbing back into bed. There was small chance I would sleep and, sure enough, I was still awake when Jess arrived home about an hour later. I heard him muttering to himself downstairs as he banged about in the living room, probably searching for his missing phone. Later I heard him at the bedroom door. He whispered, "Costa, are you awake?" I kept my breathing slow and steady, not making a sound. He searched the bedroom in places he thought he may have left his precious phone until I heard his knees crack as he kneeled to look under the bed where I had returned it.

The covers moved but I remained mute. He cursed quietly, obviously unable to see in the dark. I heard him come around to pick up my mobile, turning it on to use the light to explore under the bed. Jess's choked sound of triumph was the signal for me to start awake, yawn, and stretch. "Hello, love," I said. "Good night, was it?"

"Same old same old," he said.

My curious expression must have reminded him he was still holding my phone because he stuttered an explanation. "I found your phone in the living room. I brought it up because I thought you might need it."

"Thanks," I said with all the sincerity I could muster.

"Um…anything unusual happen tonight?" he asked. "Like…um…phone calls for me?"

"No, deathly quiet," I replied. "Simon popped in for a visit to see if we were available for a party in a few weeks. We had a few drinks. We ended up talking for hours. You know how it is when old friends catch up." Simon was my oldest friend; I'd known him since we were in junior high. "Why? Were you expecting a call?"

"No, not really. Just a friend said he might ring to see if I was working."

"Afraid not. Sorry," I lied. "What time is it?" I glanced around at the clock. "I only came to bed about two or three hours ago so I definitely would have heard his call. Surely he wouldn't have rung later than that? Anyway, even if he did, you know that once my head hits the pillow there's no waking me. Though I can't think why you didn't give him your cell phone number."

Jess kissed my forehead. "You go back to sleep. I'll just have my shower and join you shortly."

"Okay." I yawned for emphasis. "I've got a busy day tomorrow. Caz and I have a meeting with the boss." Even the semi-light of the bedroom failed to disguise the sneer on Jess's face at the mention of Caz's name. "I'll probably be late so you'll be gone by the time I get home."

"Not to worry," he said. "I have next Monday night off. Maybe we can do something special."

I mumbled, pretending I was simply too tired to discuss things further. He went into the en suite bathroom, closing the door behind him. I heard the shower but underneath it the barely audible clack of Jess sending a text message on his phone. I smiled to myself and then, satisfied, I did fall asleep.

When the alarm woke me the next morning, disturbing Jess as it always did, I kissed his eyelids, telling him to go back to sleep, while I slipped into the bathroom for my ablutions. I was happy – hysterically so – that I had a plan and that by day's end I would know for sure if my boyfriend was a serial cheat or if my imagination was in serious need of a clean-out with a wire brush.

I didn't vary my usual morning routine, having breakfast after my shower, my already chosen clothes for the day hanging in the closet downstairs so as not to wake Jess. The only variation was that I left the back door unlocked before I made an extra show of closing and locking the front door. I headed down the path and up the street toward the underground station that would whizz me into the city.

However, I doubled back as silently as possible but with enough determination in my step that if any of the neighbors saw me they would just assume that I'd gone to collect some item I'd accidentally left behind. I was hoping that Jess would not be standing at the upstairs window although I had deliberately left a folder on the coffee table as an excuse if he saw me. I slipped along the side of the house, screened sufficiently from the street that I would be unseen, quickly letting myself in the squeak-free back door.

From the kitchen I could hear that Jess was already up making plans on his cell phone, his voice carrying down the stairs as he moved about in the bedroom. Bastard! He usually set his alarm for midday. "Sorry about last night," he said. "I left my phone at home. Lucky that Costa didn't hear it ring otherwise… Yeah, stupid fucker doesn't know what day it is let alone what I get up to." His voice dropped but I could still hear him. "Yeah, I'm looking forward to it as well… I'll ring Costa at work to make sure he's there and get myself all set up. Sounds hot. My ass is twitching already… You'll be worn out just as I'm getting started. I'm insatiable, mate… Then take a fuckin' Viagra. In fact, take the whole bloody packet. Unless you hear back from me, I'll be waiting just as you instructed, Sir."

He must have disconnected the call because I heard him whistling and the thud of the bed as he obviously tidied it up for company. Then he headed into the bathroom because he left the door open and I heard the tell-tale spatter of water. Ducking back into the kitchen, I dialed work to tell them I wouldn't be in today – a touch of food poisoning – and then put the phone on vibrate. I didn't want Jess hearing the ring tone if someone called me.

I was intrigued at what Sean had set up. Not just intrigued, the situation was turning me on a little. A lot. I was hard in my trousers. Bloody angry as well that Jess was a cheating bastard who obviously had no regard for my feelings. Wouldn't know what day it was, eh? We'd soon see about that.

While Jess was in the shower I rang his cell phone. He didn't pick up so I left a message. It didn't matter either way, I was gonna have myself a big helping of revenge. "Hi, honey. You must still be asleep. I didn't want to wake you but I'm gonna be in meetings all day. Major catastrophe at one of the regional offices. You won't be able to contact me. I'll ring you when I'm coming home. Love you."

I'd just hung up from my second call when I heard Jess coming down the stairs. The safest place to hide was the pantry so I ducked inside just in time. He was obviously listening to my message because he laughed. "Stupid fucker," he spat. "You know the old expression, while the cat's away, the boyfriend will make the most of it." He made himself a coffee and while he waited poured some sugary cereal into a bowl, splashed milk over it before shoveling it into his mouth. I looked at my watch. He still had half an hour or so before Sean arrived. He scrolled through his phone and pressed dial. I wondered who he was calling.

"Hi, Jules," he said. "I feel in need of some face cream. Boyfriend is gone for the day… Yeah, I'm expecting someone at eleven but the afternoon is free… Dunno what he would do if he found out. Close call last night though."

Jesse went into detail about his cell phone mishap. He glanced at the kitchen clock. "Listen, I gotta go. This Sean dude is into role playing. Gotta get set up. Dude, bring as much face cream as you got. Get your staff…you know…Thanks, I owe ya."

He had about five minutes before Sean was due to arrive. He raced into the living room and I took a chance and crept to the door to watch. He adjusted a few cushions before positioning himself on the lounge. Obviously they were going to do it downstairs. "Shit," he cursed, running for the stairs. He'd obviously forgotten something. The only way I'd be able to watch is if I hid in the closet but that was too dangerous. I panicked. The bookcase. We'd attempted to cover the rising damp in one corner of the living room with a bookcase forming the third side of a triangle.

I was sure I could squeeze behind it. I'd have to be quick or I'd be caught. It was a tighter squeeze than I'd expected or else I'd put on weight since I'd used it as a hiding place during a party game of hide-and-seek. I also knew the thin back of the bookcase was a Swiss cheese of holes. Jesse was bounding down the stairs as I gave an almighty push and my body slid into place. He hadn't seen me. Fortunately, some of the holes were at eye height even though I had to carefully push a few of the books aside to see properly. In fact, I had three spy holes at various angles to the room.

Jesse had retrieved a large squeeze bottle of lube which he placed in a prominent position on the coffee table. He clicked on the TV and a porn movie soundtrack groaned and grunted through our home theatre sound system. The film was one I'd never seen. Jesse must have kept a stash of his favorites hidden. From what I could see, it was a gangbang movie in which a cute twink whose birthday it seemed to be was taking on a group of men at a party. Hold on, the cute twink looked awfully familiar. My stomach lurched at the recognition and I almost lost my breakfast. Jesse was the object of the gangbang. So that's what his 'student' films entailed.

Stripping his clothes off and flinging them behind the lounge, Jess stood naked for a moment ascertaining that everything was as it should be before he flipped the lid of the lube, squeezing a generous amount onto his fingers before spreading it liberally on his asshole. He wiped the residue on his own cock, giving it a perfunctory tug to get it to full strength before clicking the front door so that it was unlocked. He sank onto the lounge before hoisting his legs in the air, resting his knees on his shoulders, sliding down until his ass was easy pickings. He held his legs in place with his arms and reached around to tug his butt cheeks apart. It would be quite a sight for anyone who walked through the door. I also noticed the glint of lube as it oozed out of his hole.

About thirty seconds later, the door was pushed open and the man I assumed was Sean entered. He was nothing special, which surprised me. I thought one of the reasons Jess might feel the need to cheat was that I wasn't good-looking enough or else my body was inferior to his own sculpted masculinity. In fact, Sean was less attractive and less in condition than I was as I discovered when he silently disrobed. I thought it might have to do with cock size but, again, Sean's was about the same length and thickness as mine.

I guess that meant Jess was just a slut for cock. Anyone's cock.

Sean grinned. "That's some ass you've got there, boy. I knew as soon as I clapped eyes on it that it was gonna be mine."

Jess's cock was hard, something it rarely was when I was about to fuck him. He remained resolutely limp during our lovemaking. I obviously didn't excite him any more – if I ever did. Maybe I needed to work on my dirty talk. Wait, I didn't have any. Jess and I normally made love silently except for a grunt or two if it hurt or when I blew a load.

"I'm not fishing for compliments. Just get over here and fuck me with that big hard cock of yours," Jess demanded.

It wasn't dialogue written by an Oscar-winning script writer but it seemed to have the desired effect on Sean who barreled across the room, tugging his dick to full erection, and just slid right into Jess's hole without so much as a grimace on my boyfriend's face. The same bf who used to tell me it hurt and I might have to go without anal for a few days. The very same bf who was now being pounded into the lounge by a guy with all the finesse of a water buffalo.

"That's it, fucker, ram me hard. Make my ass hurt so I can't sit down after you blow your fuckin' load."

Sean made a few perfunctory attempts at dirty talk but seemed like he couldn't fuck and verbalize his pleasure at the same time. Mind you, it was difficult to get a word in with all the grunts, groans, fucks, slam me harders, and other expressions of sexual ardor that Jess was screaming. He was so loud I thought he should issue hearing protection to his lovers. Sean didn't seem to mind and kept up a pretty savage assault on Jess's hole. I knew the fuck Jess was copping, rough as it was, had nothing to do with punishment but my cock was hard just watching his body being pummeled into the lounge suite. I prayed it was hurting the cheating bastard and that he really wouldn't be able to sit for a week although I knew deep down it was having no such effect.

"That's it, just there. Fuck that spot." Jess wriggled his ass in an effort to guide Sean's thrusts, screaming his pleasure when the fucker's aim was true.

It was probably the reason they didn't hear the visitor. I was only aware of him because he was directly in my line of sight. Sean must have neglected to lock the front door after he came in. The new arrival made my blood curdle. It was Caz from my office. I'd never live this down as he'd take great delight in telling everyone what a cuckold I am. No, even better, he'd have photos of my cheating boyfriend being fucked senseless, screaming obscenities like a pro, as he'd captured some of the pivotal moments on his cell phone. It would be all over the net by sundown.

Once he'd filmed enough evidence of Jess's infidelity to please any jury, he cleared his throat loudly. Jess was too involved in his porn dialogue to hear it but Sean stopped mid-stroke. "What the fuck?"

"Don't stop," Jess demanded, too preoccupied with his own pleasure to realize he'd been caught.

Caz gave one of his superior smirks. "Is this a private party or can anyone join in?"

"Who are you?" Sean asked.

Jess was not about to relinquish his fuck for anyone and held Sean in place. "What do you want, Caz? Costa's not home."

"Call me psychic, but I had a sneaking suspicion after watching you for a while that he might not be. After all, he paints you as the perfect boyfriend in your, let me see, how did he phrase it? Oh, yes. In your 'totally monogamous' relationship.' I wasn't aware the Oxford Dictionary had changed its definition of 'monogamous.' I really must buy a more recent edition."

"Spare me the sarcasm, Caz. What do you want?"

"A piece of that delectable ass would be a good start."

"Not gonna happen. Why are you really here?"

"I came by to pick up an important file that's needed for an urgent meeting."

Oh, shit. My cover was about to be blown. If Caz mentioned I'd called in sick…

"Just be thankful your husband didn't come home to find you like this. Or do you now have an open relationship?"

"None of your business."

"Mm, I thought not. So Costa is clueless. Oh, I do like that." Caz tapped Sean on the shoulder. "Pray, do continue. That way I can get a few close-ups of the action."

"I said fuck off!" Jess shouted.

"I don't think so, slut boy. Not until I get a piece of that succulent ass for myself."

"Never gonna happen, sleaze bag."

"Oh, I think you may be wrong," Caz smiled. "Otherwise I may have to spill the beans to Costa. How do you think he'll react?"

"He won't believe you, shit for brains. Our relationship is built on trust."

"Keep up the abuse, boy. It'll make it all the more enjoyable when I sink my cock into your guts."

Sean interrupted our conversation. "Hey, can you two guys can it at least until I've finished. You're putting me off." He went back to pounding Jess's butthole.

Jess defiantly continued his dirty talk. "Fuck me, dude. Slam that pistol into my gaping ass. Fuck my tight little asshole."

Whether it was because he had an audience or because he wanted out of there as soon as possible, Sean picked up speed and within minutes was shuddering, obviously shooting inside Jess's raw ass. He panted until he got his breath back, and then pulled out, holding Jess's legs apart.

In the interim, Caz had shucked his clothes and was slowly rubbing his cock. It was a monster in comparison to Sean's.

Sean ran his thumb over Jess's leaking cock head. "You're drooling. You love having your ass fucked, don't you slut?"

Caz smiled as Sean rubbed his thumb up and down Jess's crack, pushing inside the glistening entrance making Jess breathe hard.

Sean was tempting Caz. "Like what you see?"

Jess attempted to wriggle free. "Fuck off, that slimeball is not getting into my ass."

"Oh, I reckon he is," Sean said. He slapped Jess's butt cheek. Hard. I heard my bf yelp at the sting. "Be a good boy and play nice with the gentleman here. I can't afford for him to post that footage of me fucking your butthole no matter how delectable it was. I'm about to be married and I have a reputation to uphold. So you do exactly what the nice man says and make us all happy."

"You piece of shit. You mongrel cunt," Jess shouted.

Caz pretended shock. "What a potty mouth. We'll have to do something about that. And such a nice mouth too. Looks like it could suck the chrome off a Cadillac fender. Still, it's not your mouth I want, tempting as it is to shut you up by stuffing big thick cock inside until you choke."

Damn, that I'd pay good money to see because Jess never took more than an inch or two. Not of mine at any rate.

"Come on, mate," Sean moaned. "Get a move on, he's wriggling like an eel and I can't hold him much longer. If you're gonna fuck him—"

"Christ!" Jess bellowed. Sean hadn't even finished the sentence before Caz sank into Jess's ass all the way to his balls. I flinched. It must have hurt. Isn't that what I wanted? The punishment to fit the crime?

Jess's dialogue had taken on a distinctly different tone now. "Not so hard. You're hurting me."

I had to hand it to Caz. He may be my nemesis but he was visiting pain and destruction better than I could. It made nonsense of Jess's demands to be fucked until he couldn't sit down for that is exactly what Caz was doing. Sean patted Jess on the head. "Thanks for the fuck, mate. Your ass is prime. Pity I can't stay longer for seconds but I can see you're occupied." He dressed while keeping an eye on the action, his cock semi-tumescent. He hovered when he was ready to go.

"Fuck off, bastard," Jess spat.

Caz didn't miss a stroke but turned his head to address Sean. "No worries, mate. I owe you. I've been after this ass for almost a year. I won't put your pic on the net. You're safe."

Sean scooted out of the house much relieved by Caz's promise.

"Now, boy, you have my undivided attention."

Jess growled.

"We can play this any way you like but I'm not taking my cock out until I spill my balls deep inside you. You can either struggle and make it a painful experience or you can lie back and enjoy it. Either way, I don't care. Then you and me are gonna have a serious discussion about how often you're gonna give up your ass to me."

"Not gonna happen. Ever."

"From what I see around here you're on a good wicket. Costa is gonna go places and he'll take you along with him provided you're a good little boy. I hear he just about supports you anyway, that crap waiter's job can't pay much unless you're selling your ass on the side."

"What do you want, Caz?"

"A sex slave would be a good start. Someone whose guts I can empty my balls in whenever I feel like it. Would make it doubly pleasurable if it was you. Cuckolding that shit boyfriend of yours who's blocking my promotion in the company. I'd have something to hold over him, something that would destroy him when I most need it."

"You're a bastard," Jess said.

"And you're a slut. It's a marriage made in heaven."

"Shut up and fuck me," Jess demanded.

I had to give Caz points for stamina. He kept at it for the next twenty minutes, varying the power of his thrusts, until Jess was begging for relief. They both came together in a howl like a gang of banshees, collapsing on the lounge in exhaustion.

"Fuck," Caz panted.

"Yeah, fuck," Jess agreed.

Even I was exhausted from just watching. And the fact I'd blown in my pants twice while being a voyeur.

"Don't get the idea I like you," Jess bitched after the most thorough fucking I think he'd ever received in his life.

"You don't have to like me," Caz replied. "In fact, it's better if you don't. Makes it more enjoyable for me." He dressed quickly, then patted Jess on the ass and left, taking the file on the coffee table. "I'll give you a call next time I need to collect a file. Maybe work on that cute cock-sucking mouth of yours."

Jess cursed loudly as Caz closed the front door. He grimaced as he wiped his ass with tissues from the box he had on the side table. "Bastard. You better not have damaged me internally," he muttered to himself as he hobbled gingerly upstairs to the bathroom. I made my escape when I heard the shower.

I caught the underground into the city and wandered the streets trying to clear my head and make sense of my life, eventually ending up at a pub where I sat quietly in a corner nursing a beer while watching raucous end of the working day businesspeople winding down before heading home. I knew I would have to do the same shortly but I didn't know how I was going to react to Jess when I saw him again. He'd ripped my heart out and trampled on it. As for Caz…

It was childish, but I wanted revenge although I had no idea how to go about it. I almost changed my mind because that night, Jess was so attentive and loving it was if he'd undergone a personality transplant.

"I've taken the night off to be with you," he said. "I've been neglecting you, Costa, and I thought I'd try and make it up to you."

He led me upstairs where he undressed and lay provocatively on the bed. "I need a shower," I complained and headed into the bathroom where I stripped off my clothes, leaning my head against the cold tiles in an effort to get my emotions in check. I'd swear that some alien had come down and swapped bodies with Jess, there was that much of a change in him. I could almost put down what I'd witnessed earlier to hallucinations if he hadn't stilled my hand as I went to penetrate his ass with my fingers.

"I wish I could, baby, but I had an attack of the runs earlier. I really wanted to, you know, but things just didn't turn out. Must have been something I ate on the job last night."

I suppose I could have confronted him at that stage but I was just so worn out emotionally I didn't have the strength. In fact, I lay on the bed after my shower and Jess did all the work, actually taking my cock farther into his mouth than he ever had before. Swallowing was still beyond him but he made an effort. Unfortunately for him, I knew it was to assuage his conscience (if he actually had one) but more as protection in case Caz revealed his indiscretion. I'm sure he'd spent most of the afternoon planning his excuses if I found out what had occurred that day. He would never admit to infidelity on an industrial scale but he was a good enough actor to beg forgiveness for one indiscretion, swearing it had never happened before and never would again, convincing me it was a momentary lapse. Sex with Caz was another matter but that he could bluff his way through. There was no footage, no photos of that. He would just deny it happened, saying that Caz was merely out to cause trouble. If Caz could somehow provide proof, then I was sure Jess would plead coercion which, to some extent, it had been.

For the following two weeks Jess was so attentive it almost became suffocating. He arrived home from work early, there were no new designer clothes or cosmetics, his cell phone was free of propositions (I checked each night after he fell asleep), and I got more sex than I had in a long while. I fucked him roughly once his ass had 'healed.' "What's got into you?" he asked with just a touch of admiration in his voice. I didn't tell him I was trying to punish him.

I was on the verge of forgiving him but I should have known his loving behavior wouldn't last. I'd been correct; it had been a ruse in case his secret life was revealed. His reversion to type began with a few new high-end label clothes, a swag of face creams, new head shots for his portfolio, and an increase in propositions on his phone. I was also back to being ignored, sex doled out as a favor whenever he had the time which suddenly became infrequent.

Caz had taken to baiting me at the office. He portrayed himself as straight and was, in fact, engaged to be married to one of the powerhouse attorneys at a law firm we used. It was certainly a step up for Caz. He always denigrated my relationship in comparison to his healthy hetero version. He didn't pretend he was or would ever be faithful to his future bride but there was also no hint that he'd porked Jess. Or that he intended doing it again.

Until I overheard a phone conversation one evening when I arrived home to find Jess in the kitchen arguing with someone. He was speaking so loudly he obviously hadn't heard me come in. I stood back to eavesdrop.

"I told you I can't. That's the one day of the year I simply can't. Why? For fuck's sake, Caz, it's my birthday. Costa always takes me out for a romantic dinner and then home for… I can't, he takes the day off. It's the one sacrosanct ritual we go through every year. Sure it's boring but what can I do? I'm not having you open my ass up with that cock of yours and then being so sore I can't perform for Costa. He'll suspect something. Fuck you, Caz. Go on, tell him then. You'll never get your dick in my ass ever again if you do that. Sure I love your cock. Why? For fuck's sake, Caz. You know why." He sighed deeply. "It's the biggest fuckin' cock I've ever had in my ass. You fuck like a dynamo. Of course you're better than Costa. No comparison. How much better? For Christ's sake, are we in kindergarten? Okay, a million times better." He was becoming annoyed. But then Caz must have said something he liked because his face lit up. "You'll what? How many guys? Fuck me." He laughed. "Yeah, I guess they will. That sounds like the sort of birthday I could really go for instead of a tedious romantic meal and a mediocre fuck afterwards. Leave it with me, I'll think of something."

I crept back to the front door, opening and slamming it as if I'd just arrived home, calling "Jess, are you awake?"

He stuck his head around the kitchen door looking somewhat startled. "Just finishing up a phone call." He put the cell phone to his ear. "Costa just got home, Jack. I don't think he'll go for it, but I'll ask. Okay? Yeah, see ya, mate."

"What was that all about?" I asked.

Jess tried his much-put-upon pout. I wasn't going to fall for that. "Jack wants me to work on my birthday."

"Not going to happen," I said.

"I told him that. He's up shit creek without a paddle. Big business do that night and he's got staff off on holidays and two down sick. He's scrambling to find good people."

"That's no concern of ours. I've been planning your birthday for months."

"I know. I know. But is there no chance you could put it off until the following night?"

Okay, now I could see where his loyalties lay. He was pissing me off big time. If I didn't get away from him to clear my head, I'd probably reveal all and that would give me no satisfaction at all. I was only part pretending when I stormed out of the kitchen and up to our bedroom where I slammed the door theatrically. That would give me a good half hour before he attempted to make amends. By the time he came in quietly, whispering "Honey, are you all right?" I'd formulated my plan.

He sat beside me on the bed, caressing my hair. "I'm sorry, babe. Of course I won't work on my birthday. I know how important it is to you. To both of us. I'll let Jack know."

As an act of good faith he blew me although I found it difficult to maintain an erection until I imagined all the men who'd been between his lips. It was perfunctory at best and he used his hands to prevent my cock from poking his tonsils. I'd had better blow jobs from a Fleshlight. I pretended an enthusiasm I felt even less than he did.

His birthday was three weeks away but I knew now what my gift would be. He'd love it.

One of the first items on my agenda was to ensure Caz and Jess got it together at least once more between now and his birthday surprise. I knew Caz was in his office, next door to mine, so I rang Jess to tell him that I'd be out of town on business the following evening. I apologized profusely but he made light of it. I hung up the phone and began the countdown. "Ten. Nine. Eight. Seven…"

I got down to five before I heard Caz's cell phone. He's a loud bastard when he's speaking, probably to big note himself, but after an effusive, "Hi. Good to hear from you," his voice became muffled so he could not be overheard. I hoped it was Jess organizing a liaison for the following evening when I was supposedly going to be away. I wasn't, of course. I was planning to hide behind the bookcase which I'd set up for my convenience. I crossed my fingers that they would perform again in the living room and not in the bedroom.

They did, Jess waiting naked and primed with his legs in the air, a somewhat drunk Caz stripping clumsily in the hallway before roughing up Jess with a stranglehold around his throat threatening dire retribution if it ever got out they were fucking. Caz wasn't hard so he forced his cock into Jess's mouth, pushing it all the way down his throat until his eyes watered and he gagged. It was a skull fuck to end all skull fucks and Jess let him know with a string of abuse once he was allowed to breathe. "You fuckin' cunt," he screamed, mucous and saliva stringing from his nose and mouth. "Don't you ever do anything like that again. I told you I don't swallow."

Caz laughed at his display of temper. "You did tonight, slut boy. And you will any time I want you to. Understand?"

Jess sulked and refused to answer. Caz got up close in his face and shouted, "Understand?" Jess nodded.

"Now turn around and put your ass in the air. That's it." Caz began to push his spongy half-hard cock against Jess's hole. "You know why I love fucking you, Jess? Cause your boy cunt is the best fuckin' cunt I ever fucked and that includes that whore I'm gonna marry. And don't think when I tie the knot I'll spare your ass, boy. I'll still be using you for my own pleasure, especially when I knock the bitch up to give me a son and heir."

Jess played the submissive well and used 'Sir' often enough that Caz eventually got hard and reamed his ass although it was a fairly lackluster fuck with only Caz getting off, leaving quickly not long afterwards, and Jess cursing in frustration. He picked up the phone and called.

"You available? I'm here all greased up and ready. You wanna come over and fuck me? Costa's out of town for the night. See you in half an hour. I'll be in the bedroom. I'll leave the door open. Let yourself in." Jess turned out the lights except for a lamp in the hallway so his guest could find his way to the stairs. I didn't need to hang around to see who it was. I no longer cared. I'd got what I wanted. I slipped out noiselessly and made my way to the hotel I'd booked for the evening where I spent a rather relaxing hour in the Jacuzzi with a rent boy I'd phoned for and who showed me more affection than I'd received from Jess in months and who had a superior technique: he swallowed and he took American Express.

About a week out from Jess's birthday I sprung my trap. I came home from work looking most forlorn. It took a while for Jess to catch on – maybe my acting wasn't up to scratch. "What's got you so grumpy?" he asked.

"Is it too late for you to tell Jack you'll work on your birthday?"

He couldn't disguise the glee in his voice. "Why? What's happened?"

"Bloody company. They're sending me interstate as a troubleshooter. The branch is not pulling its weight and they're sending me to kick ass. I can't afford to turn it down because it could mean a big promotion which means big money."

"So, they've finally woken up to what a good guy they have in you?"

"Looks that way."

"Um…how long will you be gone?"

"That's the hard part," I lied. "At least two weeks."

"Oh," he said with unalloyed delight. He must have realized because he immediately looked downcast, and added, "That long?"

"I know it's a pain but think what it will mean for us," I said. "Think what it will mean for you."

His smile was a dead giveaway.

Then I added, "You'll be able to give up that job you hate so much to concentrate on your acting career."

I doubted he was thinking of acting although he put on a memorable show of support for me including disappointment I wouldn't be home to spend time with him. "But we can celebrate when you get back. It'll be all the more…" He fumbled for the right word and then shrugged and gave up.

"Yes, it will be," I agreed.

I'd hired a car for the journey because I had a number of bags to take with me. "Why aren't you flying? Is the company that stingy?" Jess complained.

"No. I have a lot of important papers to transport, plus enough clothes and stuff." I left it vague. "Then there's the computer. I need that because it has all my important contacts and things on it." I just prayed he wouldn't look in my side of the closet. "Besides, I have a lot of planning and I need a clear head. The drive will give me an opportunity to plan my strategy."

"If it's that important, I'd be insisting on a first-class ticket and let the company pay for your luggage." Jess was such a poseur.

"Besides, I need the car for your birthday present."

That swung it. "Really? Wow, Costa, what is it?"

"Don't be impatient," I teased. "You'll have to wait a couple of days." I knew that would intrigue him.

On the big morning I woke him to wish him a happy birthday. He was groggy with lack of sleep and mumbled his thanks. "I'll ring you when I can," I said before kissing him on the forehead. "You take care. Try to enjoy your birthday without me."

"I don't know how I will," he muttered.

He was lying. He knew perfectly well how he'd enjoy his big day.

I went downstairs, glancing about the house we'd shared the best part of a year. It no longer felt like home. I made a show of slamming the car doors and driving off in a flurry of exhaust. However, I parked in a nearby dead-end side street where no one would see me and then I walked back to the house as inconspicuously as possible, hoping that Jess had not gone downstairs as yet. It usually took him about fifteen minutes to wake up properly.

I let myself in and took up my position behind the bookcase. It had become like a home away from home. Not long after I'd settled, Jess came downstairs in his boxer shorts, scratching his balls. He was on the phone already. He pinched his nose; an old trick to make him sound like he was all stuffed up and nasally. "Listen, Jack. I've come down with some virus or the other. Really sick." He coughed to labor the point. He was usually a better actor than this. "Called the doctor over to check me out… Yeah, there are doctors who still make house calls…Anyway, he says I gotta take the rest of the week off… Of course, I've got a certificate. Says I'm highly contagious. You don't want some corporate bigwig or a bridal party coming down with what I've got. It's coming out both ends."

Nice touch, I thought. That should do it. Sure enough, Jess told Jack he'd ring with an update later in the week.

So far, Jess had acted exactly as I'd expected. Not that it would have thwarted my plans if he hadn't. He had a leisurely breakfast while texting or ringing people to come over to help him celebrate throughout the day and night. And I suspect throughout the two weeks I was scheduled to be away. He went upstairs to shower having made the first appointment for the early afternoon. I knew he'd go out and bring home loads of alcohol and nibbles. I texted my contact. Half an hour later, the doorbell rang.

Jess came stumbling down the stairs in a new pair of boxers and smelling of so much soap and after shave I could smell him across the room. "Who the fuck is this?" he muttered as he flung open the door.

"You Jess?" a gruff voice asked.

"Yes," he replied.

"I've got something for you. Can I bring it in?"

"Sure." He could scarcely keep the excitement out of his voice.

"Okay, Vince, this is the house. Bring her in." He came into the living room. "We were told to set it up here."

"What is it?" Jess asked.

"We were told not to reveal it until we'd set it up. Okay?"

"I guess. Who sent it?"

The guy handed him an envelope which Jess tore open like a little kid. "It just says here it's from an ardent admirer."

Vince pushed a number of large cardboard cartons into the hall on a trolley. "Where you want this stuff, Abe?"

"Instructions are to set it up in the living room."

"Shit, eh? Someone's gonna have some fun."

"It's my birthday," Jess informed them. "Could be anyone."

Abe laughed. "Modest, eh?"

"Someone must have it bad for you, mate," Vince said, cutting open the boxes.

Jess was on tenterhooks waiting to see what he'd been sent, still oblivious to what it was as the two men constructed the secure metal frame. Vince swung from the top beams to ensure it could support his weight.

"What the fuck is it?" Jess asked.

"Patience, mate. All will be revealed."

They hung the chains, the cuffs, and then Abe turned to the final box.

Jess looked as if all his birthdays had come at once. "Holy shit, is this what I think it is?"

Vince chuckled. "Don't know what you think it is, mate, so I can't tell you."

Soon the entire structure was completed. The three men stood back to admire it.

"Must have cost a packet," Vince said.

"Top of the range," Abe agreed.

"A fuckin' sling," Jess cooed in admiration.

"Okay, hop up in it," Abe ordered. "We have to adjust it for height."

Jess was all too eager, swinging himself onto the leather sling, getting comfortable by putting his hands on the chains that held it up.

"Here, you'll be more comfortable if you put your hands in these. They're padded," Vince advised.

Suspecting nothing, Jess allowed his wrists to be secured in padded cuffs.

"Now your legs. Hoist them up here a bit," Abe said, helping to secure Jess's ankles. "Now, let's see if it's the right height." Abe stood at crotch height to Jess's ass. "Can't really tell with your undies on. Got your knife handy, Vince?" Vince handed it over and Abe cut the boxers from Jess's body. "Nice cock, you got there, son. You got the rest of the birthday present, Vince?"

"Sure do, buddy."

"Hand me the cock ring. You do his nipples."

"What's going on here?" Jess was beginning to panic.

"Take it easy, mate." Abe stroked Jess's cock which calmed him down just enough that he could snap the leather cock ring tightly around Jess's defenseless cock and balls. Jess was so preoccupied with that he didn't notice Vince about to snap alligator clips on his nipples. I'm sure his cry of pain could be heard down the street.

"The height looks right," Vince said. "But there's only one real way to tell."

"You're right, mate. Pass me the lube."

Abe undid his work pants and dropped them and his briefs, pulled his shirt up over his belly and smeared his cock with the lube Vince had handed him. He also smeared some gel on Jess's ass, pushing his fingers inside. "He's fuckin' tight for a slut," Abe said admiringly.

"Get on with it. Test him for height."

Jess looked on in amazement as the delivery guy lined up his cock with his ass and pushed his way in. He wasn't gentle and Jess writhed to get away from the invasion. "Exactly the right height for me, Vince. But you should try it after me to make sure it's comfortable for you as well."

Jess began cursing as Abe thrust powerfully in and out of his ass, the sling having just enough give to make it comfortable. "Hot ass, mate. No wonder your buddies want you strung up and ready."

Jess was attempting to break free. "Get the fuck off me. I'll have your jobs for this. Fuckin' cunts."

"Quite a mouth on him," Vince said. "I'd love to stop it with my cock but I'm afraid he might bite."

"Use the clamp, that's what it's for."

"You mean this?" Vince said holding up a wire contraption.

Jess looked horrified. "No, please. I'll be good."

Vince and Abe looked at each other. "Nah, we don't trust you."

Before Jess could call for help, Vince had wired Jess's mouth open so a man could insert his cock and Jess would have no opportunity to bite him. Once it was in position, Vince slid his cock between Jess's stretched lips. "Hot throat."

It took the men about half an hour of constant checking Jess's ass and throat before they were satisfied that the apparatus had been set up correctly. They'd both also deposited two loads in Jess's ass and mouth.

Slapping him on the butt, they both wished him a happy birthday before blindfolding him and leaving him strung up like a Christmas turkey. Once they'd left, I came out of my hiding place. Jess could hear movement but he had no idea who was with him or where they'd come from. I walked to the hallway and took off my business suit and placed a leather hood over my face, removing the riding crop I'd secreted against my leg.

I opened and closed the front door as if I'd just arrived. Jess shivered in fear, unable to extricate himself from the situation. I removed the blindfold so he could see me although there was no flicker of recognition. My cock was revenge hard and I took great delight in pulling his head back to insert my cock in his mouth, pushing until I hit his gag reflex. He bucked as I entered his throat, holding his face against my groin until I thought I'd shoot from the sheer pleasure it gave me to be all the way inside him for once. But I withdrew because I had other things in mind.

I ran the tip of the riding crop across his chest and down his abs to his cock which I flicked to Jess's scream of pain before repeating the exercise a little less viciously on his sensitive balls. His cock oozed a thick string of pre-cum. He was enjoying it.

I swatted his ass, Jess wriggling in the sling to escape the blows, until his cheeks were red, varying it by sometimes beating his nipples and his stomach. I was enjoying myself, my cock harder than it had been for months. I didn't want to torture Jess, it was merely punishment so it had to hurt a little. It's not in me to be a sadist so eventually I tired of the game. I fucked his face a little, lubricating my cock with his saliva, before standing between his legs and shoving my cock into his anus. He groaned as I gripped his thighs, fucking my frustration away as if he were a slab of meat.

I removed the metal device from his mouth – I didn't want him choking – and kissed him brutally. It would be the last time. He welcomed me, sucking on my tongue, pushing his ass back against my invading prick. The fucker was getting off on it. He squealed when I removed the nipple clamps, the blood rush stinging him. I pinched his buds until he begged for mercy, all the while impaling him on my cock.

Eventually, I could stand no more. I grabbed his throat roughly and banged his ass until I shot my load as he begged me to fuck harder. I slumped over him until I gained my breath back.

"Who are you?" he asked. "That was the best fuck I've had all year."

He said that to everyone. No matter. It was over. I walked to the hallway still in disguise. I dressed out of his sight while he yelled, "Hey, don't go. Let me out of this thing. Help me."

I had no intention of letting him free. I left the hood and the other toys where they could be found. Letting myself out the door, I was careful to leave it unlocked, knowing he would have a steady stream of admirers ready to use his ass and his throat for the rest of the day until, intrigued by a suggestive text, Jack, his boss, would turn up to have a turn. The listing I'd put on gay social media calling for men to share their spunk with Jess for his special day – turn up and dump a load – was sure to attract men of all shapes and sizes. As long as they had a cock, I didn't think Jess would complain.

I unlocked the car and without looking back drove out of the city. In a few hours Caz's fiancée would receive a parcel with video evidence of her boyfriend fucking my ex, all the dialogue beautifully captured along with the digital vision. Caz's boss would also receive a similar package which should put paid to his career with the company. Once Jess was released from the sling in a day or two, he would discover that I was gone, my side of the closet bare. Anything I had left behind he was welcome to keep. He would also discover that I had emptied our bank account – it was mainly my money anyway although I'd left him just enough to get by for a month if he was frugal while he looked for a new place to stay. I'd canceled the credit cards and paid the bills until the end of the month.

I had a new job in a new state. I was starting over. As I drove away from the city that had been my home for most of my life, heading across the river toward the freeway, I tossed Jess's cell phone into the water, mine following shortly after.

Bloody cell phones. They'd almost destroyed my life.

I WAS A MALE NYMPHO FOR THE FBI

Casebook Log #369

You know how humiliating it is to assume the position against a cop car, your shorts down around your ankles, your tackle flapping in the breeze, while a deputy gives you the once over before fat Sheriff Tucker covers his podgy fingers in a rubber glove to inspect your anal area for drugs?

It was such a fuckin' buzz, and I loved it. Plus, I had them right where I wanted them.

I'd been hitchhiking along the interstate A380, stripped to the waist to show off my hot abs and ceps; my pecs and back awash with perspiration, my shorts barely hiding my fat sausage of a cock. See, I get turned on when I display myself like this. I'm an exhibitionist at heart. Hell, there ain't much that I'm not when it comes to things sexual.

My ass is my best asset, so my cut-off jeans were way too revealing – cut so that half my ass cheeks were on display. I was – I am – hot, hot, hot! I attracted attention just the way I like it. A couple of guys drove around in circles to get a gander at me to make sure I was for real. You seldom saw what I was offering outside a porn movie. A couple of the more adventurous, or more horny, guys pulled over to see if I wanted a lift. Any driver who looked as if he was packing got my attention. And my ass or my mouth later, if he wanted them. Who am I kidding? They always wanted them. It was the only reason they picked me up. I didn't need a lift and their concern for my comfort and welfare was anything but altruistic.

Like I'm complaining?

I could have made a fortune because most of my pick-ups thought I was on the game and their first question after "You need a lift?" and my response, "Nah, I need a fuck" once I'd hopped in their car, was usually, "How much?" When I told them it was all free they couldn't believe their luck, especially the guys sporting wedding rings. Even more so the guys who were a little on the homely side or else putting on the weight. You see, I'm an equal opportunity fuck. Just about insatiable. As long as it's male and has a cock, preferably on the largish size – but even that doesn't matter – I'm available. Solo, double acts, or groups. You name your poison. Not that anyone's died yet from sampling my wares, although a few have had heart palpitations from the exertion of trying to satisfy me.

I knew I'd eventually attract the attention of the authorities. I was causing all sorts of traffic infringements as guys, and an almost equal number of women, slowed down to ogle the booty. The ladies were out of luck.

I noticed the cop car trailing me just far enough back they thought they were invisible, and stepped up my slutty behavior, wiggling my luscious buns even more blatantly at the passing parade. My training meant I had a second sense when it came to being followed. I was encouraging it. I wanted to provoke the cops but it seems I'd have to be more outrageous. I stopped and flexed, showing off my body even more blatantly, bending over to open my knapsack to retrieve my water bottle so that my ass spread invitingly for speeding voyeurs, the thin strip of fabric between my cheeks barely covering my twitching hole. If passers-by looked closely enough they'd probably see the sun reflected off the snail trail of dried spunk glistening in and around my butt hole.

Does it get any better than that?

Time to introduce myself properly. I'm special agent Vic Tulsa, I'm twenty-five years old, handsome as fuck (I think I already said that), hot hairless bod kept in shape by vigorous sexual workouts and the gym, and with the help of depilatory wax for the stray hairs around my butt hole. When I'm not working you'll usually find me working out – my muscles or my sexual organs. I really gotta get me a life. I suppose you could call me a sex addict – as long as you call me.

That's not why I was chosen for the job. The other guys at FBI headquarters don't know about my love of all things perverse. In fact, other sex addicts can only dream of the things I get up to all legal and above board. Plus I get paid to do them.

Pity they gave me that asshole, Ted Hass, who liked to big note himself as Bad Hass around HQ, as my boss. He's so buttoned up that sometimes I think people might mistake him for a shirt. He's more hindrance than help. He cramps my style. You see, I'm a bit flamboyant, a bit in your face. What I'm trying to say is: my style is gay, gay, gay. And Ted, no shit, is an arch homophobe. Doesn't believe the FBI should be employing perverts – his word not mine.

Naturally, in an industry as macho and competitive as the FBI, every male on the job has to scratch his balls at least five times every hour just to let you know how masculine he is. Or when I'm around they scratch their balls big time as if it releases a hetero testosterone that repels gay men. Yeah, like any of them are beddable. I know the other agents are saying stuff behind my back that would get them a new set of teeth and nose realignment if they said it to my face. What can I do about it?

Worst is Bluto Sanchez, named for the bully from the Popeye cartoons. He's a fuckin' mountain of a man, even in a suit. He's usually sent on jobs that require intimidation or muscle. Seldom does he get jobs that require any sort of mental capacity. Me they send on jobs that no one else will handle. First, I'm single, and married guys never get the really shitty jobs. Second, my boss thinks gay men have nothing but sex on their mind constantly. In my case, that's true, but he doesn't know that, he's just pandering to clichés. Third, ergo, any sex crimes that are downright sleazy and nasty should be a piece of cake for someone with my interests.

I baulked getting all the psychosexual crimes at first, not wanting to get a reputation, but what the hell, it turned out I was good at it. I was especially good at it when I worked alone and went undercover. I got results where other agents on the job got killed, maimed, or psychiatric confinement. Of course, I bent the rules, and I didn't have to play act in some of the seedier subcultures of society – I felt right at home. If I had to get laid in the pursuit of my enquiries, well, it didn't go into my reports. No one cared as long as I got results.

Well, almost no one cared. Ted Hass cared. Bluto Sanchez cared. A few other guys cared as well but they weren't as in my face as the two I just mentioned. Didn't help that I called the boss Ted Ass to his face, especially amongst those sucking his balls for promotion – not literally, of course, as I'm sure his balls were as dry as the skin on his wrinkled old face. I did recommend a moisturizer once but he just screamed about fags so I let it go. Who cares that the skin on his forehead flakes off like ice floes splitting from the main glacier in Iceland? Ted sure doesn't. I dread the days he tosses over a report because it's usually covered in shredded skin.

Just like the one he handed me that day. I knew it was a beauty when he said, "The big boys upstairs think you're the only man for the job." He screwed his face up, so I knew he was lying. He was an old-fashioned martinet who did things by the book. He couldn't help himself whenever he saw me in the labyrinthine corridors of the Quantico building in West Virginia. He'd railed against accepting gay men, lesbians, transgender and bisexual agents. It was obvious by the way he assigned the worst jobs to anyone who had the balls to come out. As a result there were a lot of closet cases in the Bureau. I was not one of them.

Hass attempted to beat the gay out of me or have me assassinated by an enemy power on numerous occasions, all to no avail. It galled him when I kept popping up like a bad penny. I could just imagine his delight when the latest case landed on his desk. "This sounds like a case made in heaven for you, Mr. Tulsa."

I flipped through the pages, giving them a cursory glance. "Why is this case of interest now? It goes back years. You didn't want me investigating a few months back. So what's changed?"

That gave him the signal to pontificate. Nothing he liked better. "Who cares if good-for-nothing hitchhikers get themselves disappeared? Not our responsibility. They're either dead now or drug-fucked, selling themselves to feed their habit. Dunno how many times you have to tell young people today…" He was about to launch into another one of his tirades about the youth of today and their lack of morals and their lack of respect for their elders, especially one Ted Hass.

"Spare me the lecture, Hass. I know your problems with the youth of today and it don't cut no ice with me. Why is this case that's so cold it has icicles hanging off the damn pages so important now?"

One of the perks of being good at my job is I could give the old man lip. And if in so doing I gave him a massive coronary, so much the better. I knew this case was gonna be the pits.

Hass almost smirked as he revealed the details. "Normally we'd not be interested in a small case like this. There's a sheriff, Tucker I think his name is, who's Johnny-on-the-spot. Good man. Good Christian. Great help to the FBI on occasions. He reckons these kids want to disappear. Runaways and tragics, can't get their act together because of drugs, booze, perverted sex, and don't bother letting their families know if they're all right."

"What you're not saying here, Ted," I made myself comfortable without having been asked, "is that you want me on the case because it's more dangerous than you're willing to admit, it's about sex, no one else wanted it, but mostly because there's a good chance I'll wind up one of the missing."

He spluttered until saliva ran down his chin, but didn't bother to deny my accusation. I'd respect the old bastard more if he just came out and told the goddam truth for a change.

The case involved a series of young men who disappeared on a stretch of the highway between Acacia

Creek and the large town of Edsol. It was the purview of the aforementioned Sheriff Tucker, a fat slug of a man who reigned over his territory like a medieval lord. The FBI and the state authorities had tried (and failed) to pin charges on him, from drug syndication through to bribery, without success. The hottest lawyers in the country were in his pocket and he managed to slither his way out of every single charge. For once I'd been passed over and other agents were already handling the case. "I thought Danzer and Picton were on this?"

Hass shifted uncomfortably in his seat. "They've gone missing."

Danzer and Picton were new guys out to make their mark and, because they sucked up to Hass, they got the undercover job. I'd wanted it bad. Good looking dudes go missing? It had to be a gay crime. Or a gay hate crime. Either way, I was itching for it. Nah, Hass in his infinite wisdom gives it to two guys greener than the grass on a manicured golf course.

I turned a few pages of the file before I looked up and asked, "Whereabouts in here does it query the decision of the commanding officer to send in rookies who didn't even know how to scratch their pubic lice? That I want to read."

Hass turned purple in the face as he did every time I baited him.

"You will not disrespect your fellow agents," he bellowed.

I smiled reasonably, keeping my voice neutral. "How come that doesn't work when it comes to respecting this fellow agent?" I took a notebook out of my coat pocket.

He snorted. "I don't know what you're talking about."

"For example, just last week Sanchez said, and I quote, 'Tulsa should watch himself or one of these days someone will stick the barrel of their gun up his butt and blow his anal cunt apart. And that person might be me. I hate faggots.' And then there's…" I gave him six examples of threats or verbal abuse from the previous four weeks. He went to interrupt, but I silenced him when I held my hand up. He could see I meant business. "Or this little gem. Again, I quote. 'If I could find a case that would guarantee the fag would never come back alive, my problems would be over.' I guess you don't need three guesses as to who said that." I closed the notebook and put it back in my pocket.

"You've got no proof," Hass said smugly.

"You think you'd still have a job behind that desk if I did?"

"What are you gonna do with your pissy little notebook?"

I leaned in conspiratorially. "Just between you and me, Ted," he flinched when I used his first name, "What's in my little notebook will be all over the net as well as copies sent to every decent newspaper and television news service if I turn up dead at any time between now and my retirement."

"How did you get information about my private conversation?" Typical of the man. No apology, no embarrassment, just self-preservation. He grabbed the phone and demanded a team come and sweep his office for bugs. As he put the phone down he looked at it suspiciously. Good, I'd made him paranoid. It would drive him nuts when he discovered his office was contamination free.

Have you ever noticed it's always the gay guy who gets the short straw when it comes to working on public holidays, or gets the shit jobs, or gets put into danger for the sake of the greater good? And that brings us to our story.

"This Tucker guy is my contact?" I asked.

"Nope. Orders from above are that you and you alone are to hitch along the stretch of highway where the men were last seen, suss out what you can. It's no ordinary operation."

"No shit, Sherlock," I said sarcastically, wishing he'd get to the point.

"The Edsol sheriff's department sent some undercover girls out on the road but all they got for their trouble was a lot of kinky propositions. Nothing concrete. We need ourselves a male slut who knows how to flaunt it. Funnily enough, Tulsa, I thought of you. I wonder why?"

"Same reason that whenever I think of miserable old bastards your face flashes in my mind. The profile fits."

He turned red as a ripe raspberry.

"So why the urgency in this case now," I asked, tapping the folder in my lap.

"Ah, let me see." He fumbled through the papers and files on his desk until he found a newspaper clipping. He tossed it across the desk. It was a small report obviously buried on the inside pages of a small-town newspaper with limited circulation. Anyone else would have made a big deal out of it because this was explosive news. "No reports of this in the big papers or TV news."

"Authorities are sitting on it. Only leaked in that Assholeville News because the town is miniscule and, well, there's fuck all else news to report and you have to fill the paper with something."

I whistled. The gist of the three paragraph story was that local college boy, Tyson Bridgewood, had seemingly gone missing while on a charity walk across the country to raise awareness of the lack of care facilities for the disabled in his state. It would have been unremarkable given the number of young people who disappear each year except for a number of salient points that would have escaped the notice of general readers. Young Tyson was handsome as fuck and built like the proverbial if the photograph of him stripped to the waist at a local fishing competition was anything to go by. "Recent photo?" I asked.

"Taken a few days before he set out on his goddamned save-the-retards trek."

I made another entry in my notebook, much to Hass's chagrin. It was more effective than a lecture.

The second salient point was that the last time anyone heard from Tyson was from his cell phone which pinpointed his position as just outside Edsol. But the most prominent point, unmentioned in print because the locals at whom the story was aimed would have been familiar with it, was that Tyson was the only son of rabid right-wing Republican Senator and Christian Fundamentalist, Mathias Bridgewood, who espoused opinions so extreme that more moderate Christians were repelled by them. Nice piece of work.

"What do we know about this Tyson boy?" I screwed my face up. "What sort of man calls his son Tyson?"

Hass didn't bother answering the second part of the question. It was rhetorical anyway. "Apart from the fact he was a rabble rouser at university—"

"Can we have less of the moral editorializing and more facts? I want to get a grip on the situation. What the fuck does rabble rousing mean?"

"He was very political on campus. Mainly left-wing causes. Women's rights, gay rights, African-American rights—"

"The antithesis of his dad." I was speaking aloud for my own benefit, not Hass's. "Criminal record?"

"None. But that could be because of his father's influence."

"Do we know if the son is gay?"

"Oh, for God's sake, Tulsa—"

"It's relevant to the case, Hass. Get off your priggish high horse and come down to earth. The guys who have all gone missing, including Danzer and Picton, are all buff and good-looking. And I'd bet the shirt off my back there's been no ransom demand for young Tyson." Hass shook his head. "How long has he been missing?"

"Two months."

"Christ, Hass. Who the fuck has been sitting on this case for two fucking months?" He merely looked defeated. "If I save your ass on this, there better be an attitude change in this department. Now, do we know for sure that young Bridgewood didn't just get jack of his dad's conservative bullshit and simply disappear?"

Hass squirmed in his seat. "We've all but ruled it out. Young Bridgewood left with a knapsack, a change of clothes, a small amount of cash and a little food and water. His ATM card hasn't been used since the day of his disappearance. He wasn't alone, but the others in the group—"

"There were others?"

"That's what I just said. A group of five or six others, mainly girls. Groupies of young Bridgewood, it's reported."

"By whom?"

"Um, by Bridgewood Senior, if I remember correctly."

"So we can discard that bullshit straight off. What about that sheriff? Tucker? What's his story?"

"It was evening when the youngsters got to the outskirts of the town according to Tucker. He'd just been contacted by a local who was concerned about such a large group of 'hippies' I think they were described as. He and his deputy, man by the name of Forbes, drove out to take a look. When the group leader explained their purpose it seems Tucker told them to keep walking and get out of his jurisdiction as fast as their legs would carry them. It was only later the group noticed young Bridgewood was no longer with them. They tried his mobile but it went to voicemail. They kept walking, thinking he would catch up, that he'd fallen behind for some unknown reason, like he was taking a shit in the bushes, that sort of thing. They didn't report his disappearance until the following day."

"Was Tucker shown a photo of Tyson Bridgewood?"

"First thing. He denied ever seeing the boy. Swore Bridgewood wasn't with the group when he'd stopped to question them. None of the college kids could swear for certain Bridgewood was with them at the time."

I'd heard enough. "Right. I want a one-on-one interview with the Senator and tell him if he tries to shovel bullshit he can get another patsy to carry the can for this fuck-up. Otherwise you can get Sanchez or one of the others on it."

"You know they won't—"

"Tough shit!" I left the office, my smile of satisfaction unnoticed by Hass as he picked up the phone, glancing at it suspiciously.

****

If they ever remake *Gone with the Wind* then Bridgewood's palatial home is almost a certainty for Tara. When I arrived at the front of the mansion a butler opened the door before I even had a chance to ring. Perhaps they didn't want me sullying their paintwork. The servant's attitude was neutral as I was led along olde world hallways adorned with fusty oil paintings of ugly relatives adding to the gloom.

At the end of the passageway, the butler stopped to knock on an aged oak door. An authoritative voice called, "Enter." The butler opened the door and ushered me in wordlessly. A middle-aged man in an expensive suit gave me the once over from his chair behind a desk that dwarfed any I had ever seen before. It must have been constructed from a forest of trees. "Ah, Mr. Tulsa, please be seated."

The Senator made no effort to stand or to shake my hand. I dragged an old armchair closer to his desk, scuffing the floor as I did so. Bridgewood merely seemed amused. "I was warned about you, Mr. Tulsa."

"I expected you would be, Senator."

"You want to know about my son?"

"It will help the investigation."

"You don't believe he was kidnapped?"

"The only thing I can say with any certainty is that he was not kidnapped for ransom."

"What other sort of kidnap is there?"

"The list is endless. In your case it could be blackmail, an effort to gain your support for controversial legislation, or perhaps he's been sold in sexual slavery." I allowed him to think about it for a moment before asking, "Is your son gay?"

He must have been warned about my questions as well. "I don't see the relevance, Mr. Tulsa."

"It's not your job to see the relevance, Senator," I said without rancor. I wasn't about to be intimidated by some puffed-up windbag. "Do I need to repeat the question?"

He sighed in resignation. "They say you're the best so I suppose I have no choice if I want the job done properly." He leaned forward and his face took on a nasty demeanor. "But, let me tell you something young man, if you fuck up, I will not only hang you out to dry, I will have your balls pureed for my morning smoothie and you will never work anywhere in this goddamned universe ever again."

"May I quote you, Senator?" I took my notebook out of my pocket.

"Ah, the pocket notebook. It doesn't scare me, Mr. Tulsa."

"It's not meant to, Senator. It's merely to jog my memory when it comes to payback time. Now, for the third and final time, let's get back to the question which you seem so keen to avoid."

"The simple answer is that I don't know. We don't exactly have a close father/son relationship. As your research undoubtedly already informed you, we are both somewhat embarrassed by the each other's political positioning. Whereas he is of the extreme left, I am—"

"So far to the right that even your fellow Republicans find your posturing embarrassing."

I give him credit, he kept his cool. "I was going to say, I am of the middle conservative ground. It's not called the 'right' for nothing, Mr. Tulsa."

"Fine by me, Senator, because I won't, as you so eloquently put it, 'fuck up.' It goes without saying that when I return Tyson to you, always assuming he wants to return, I will make a big noise about how a member of a minority group you pillory constantly was the one who saved your offspring."

"That will never happen," he said coldly. "I have contacts in the news media."

"The conservative news media," I corrected him. I felt bad about what I was about to say but the bastard really irked me and I wanted the grip I had on his balls to tighten until he squirmed. "Your son's life is in my hands, Senator. I would hate to report that he became collateral damage in our fight against organized crime."

He didn't flinch. "I would appreciate that outcome, Mr. Tulsa, if you were to find that his sexual persuasion was as far removed from mine as his politics."

Perhaps the old bastard was playing a game of double bluff hoping that as a gay man I would do everything in my power to save one of my 'brothers.' Nah, I dismissed the thought; Senator Bridgewood was thinking only of his own political skin. I felt unclean just talking to him. I rose from my chair. "I have all I need. Thank you for your time." I didn't offer my hand. He didn't either. I made my way to the door where the butler was waiting to escort me to the front door. I could not even begin to imagine what it must be like living in this antique mausoleum.

As he was about to close the door behind me, the butler said softly, "Don't judge the Senator too unkindly, Mr. Tulsa. For all his bluster, he genuinely cares for his son."

Going on the premise that servants know more of the goings on in great mansions than their masters, I asked. "Is Tyson gay?"

"To the best of my knowledge, he's not, sir."

The butler closed the door in my face.

****

Sheriff Tucker was fingering my butthole as painfully as he could make it, almost shoving his entire fist inside me. He was a sadistic bastard, prolonging my humiliation at the side of the highway in full view of passing traffic, little realizing I was so turned on I was in danger of blowing a load. Self-control was never one of my strong points and it was only with considerable effort that I stopped myself from groaning, forcing myself to feign revulsion.

Sure, Deputy Forbes was a hot piece of cock if the bulge in his tight uniform was anything to go by. It was growing by the minute as he watched Tucker attack my ass. "Go easy, Sheriff," he warned. "You don't want to ruin him for later."

Later? That sounded ominous.

"Lookie. What have we here?" the sheriff gloated. "So that's what you've been up to. It'll be a long stretch in prison for you, my boy."

I knew before I turned to look that he was holding up a small plastic bag of some dangerous drug. Not because

I'd hidden it in my rectum but because it's what cops plant as evidence when they think they can get away with it. It was just as obvious it hadn't been anywhere near my anal tunnel because it was dry as the Gobi Desert, whereas anything that had been in my warm and snuggly would have been coated with the globs of spooge still inside me.

"You're under arrest for carrying prohibited drugs in a quantity large enough to prove you were selling. Deputy."

My arms were wrenched behind my back and Deputy Forbes cuffed my wrists. I pretended indignation. Hass's whitewash of Tucker because of his faith carried no weight with me. It was obvious he had something to do with the disappearances even if he wasn't directly responsible himself. The only way to find out was to deliver myself to his clutches. From what I'd seen so far, Tucker was as corrupt as a month-old maggot-ridden cadaver.

I was shoved into the back seat of the cop car and driven off, supposedly to my humiliation. A number of passing vehicles honked, whether in support of me or the sheriff I wasn't sure. The two law enforcement officers were so self-satisfied I really wanted to rub their noses in how easy it was to escape them. Any self-respecting criminal could have got away with ease, so for a trained FBI agent it would have been a piece of cake. However, I leaned back in the seat to wait, my ass still tingling from the intrusion of the sheriff's fat, stubby fingers, wishing I had something more fulfilling in my butt.

Back at the cop station, one of those generic one-story non-descript brick buildings that appear as substantial as a pig's straw house, I did my best whimpering act. "Don't put me in the cells. Please. I'll do anything."

"Lock him up, deputy," Tucker said maliciously.

I struggled and begged to the best of my acting ability as Forbes attempted to drag me away. I must have been convincing because Tucker back-handed me across the face making my lip bleed. "Grow some balls, son," he spat. "Get used to the cells because after what we found on you, you'll be spending a very long holiday in one. And by the looks of that ass on you, you'll be very popular."

"You're not wrong there, sheriff," Forbes agreed.

I allowed myself to be tugged into the adjoining cell area, my face wet with sniveling. When Forbes took the cuffs off, I wiped my nose on the back of my hand. "What's gonna happen to me?" I wailed.

"That all depends on you," he drawled. "You can make it easy on yourself by giving the sheriff what he wants."

"And if I don't?"

"Then you're looking at a long stretch. We don't take kindly to drugs in this town."

"Unless they're in the sheriff's possession to plant on unsuspecting hitchhikers."

"Now, see, that attitude ain't gonna make you no friends. I suggest you have a good think," he tapped my head as if I didn't know where my brain was, "and calm down. Won't do you no good mouthing off about Sheriff Tucker. He's well regarded in this town. In the entire district. Judge won't take too kindly if you bad mouth a good man. Get my drift."

"I think so," I replied miserably.

After Forbes locked me in, he headed back to the main office. There were three cells but, apart from mine, they were empty. However, I didn't think it would be my home for very long. I lounged on the lumpy single mattress on what passed for a bed but no sooner had I made myself comfortable than Sheriff Tucker came into the cell area, locking the door behind him. "Well, boy, had a chance to think things over?"

"Yes, sir," I said, although I had no idea what I was supposed to be thinking about. My mind had been on cock.

"What have you decided?"

"I'll do anything if you'll let me go."

"Glad to hear it.

He unlocked my cell, leaving the door ajar. "Don't even think about it, boy. You won't get far even if you could get past Deputy Forbes. Now, drop them itsy bitsy shorts you got on, son. Then get down on your knees like you was prayin' in church."

I was up off the bed and obeying his instructions before he had a chance to pull down the zipper on his trousers. I sank to my knees in front of him. "Ever chow down on a thick piece of man meat?" he asked.

D'uh. Why the fuck did he think I was dressed like a two-bit whore, jumping in and out of strange men's cars? He knew I wasn't carrying drugs of any description so…wasn't it obvious?

I played along. "No, sir. That's disgusting." I didn't add what I was thinking, *And downright gross in your case.*

I was face height with the sheriff's belly overhang. I had to give credit where it's due, he had a fine piece of thick, long man meat poking out from under his belly, plus a nice set of dangling balls. "Like what you see, fag?"

"It's a mighty fine cock, sir," I complimented. "But there's no way I can fit all that in my mouth."

"I'm sure you'll get it all down your throat if you want me to let you go."

"You drive a hard bargain, sir."

"Just remember, all the cards are stacked in my favor."

Tentatively, I reached for the sheriff's cock, touching it quickly before pulling my hand away as if it were hot as molten steel.

"Get your mouth around it. Quit stalling."

I closed my eyes so he could see I wasn't happy with his cock anywhere near my mouth, then leaned forward to lick the glistening purple knob, shuddering theatrically as if it was the most perverted thing I had ever done when, in reality, I just wanted to sink the beautiful prick all the way down my throat.

He groaned when he felt my tongue touch his glans. Slowly I licked along the shaft, his cock twitching in excitement, before making my way back to the knob to engulf it between my lips. I wasn't going to let him get it all his own way. I suddenly spat his cock out of my mouth. "It's gross. I can't do it."

"Oh, you'll do it all right. And you'll be begging for more by the time I've finished with you." So saying, he pinched my nostrils together so I'd eventually have to breathe through my mouth. When I opened up, he rammed his cock in as far as it would go. I choked, although I could easily accommodate his dick, no matter that it was larger than average. I scraped the sensitive skin of his shaft with my teeth. "Watch it, boy. No teeth. If you do that again, you might find a few of them knocked out of your head before the day's over. Get my meaning."

I shook my head.

"Good boy, now try again."

This time I slowly slid my lips around his prick, sliding all the way down to his balls, taking him in my throat. The sheriff was so stupid if he thought a novice could do that without gagging. I bobbed a few times to give him some idea of the pleasure he was in for before attacking his balls with my tongue. "Oh, God," he moaned. "Nobody's ever done that before." I licked and sucked his scrotum until he was writhing in excitement. I didn't want him to come like that, I wanted his cock in my mouth when he blew his load. I felt the clutch in his nuts, so I quickly put my lips over his nozzle and syphoned like the devil. He placed his hands on the back of my head to hold me still and then skull fucked the shit out of my throat. It's not the perfect way for the guy on his knees to enjoy oral, but, hey, I was getting off on it. Tucker's cock was sticky with drool and pre-cum as he pulled out, before he sank his prodigious prick all the way in again. He repeated the exercise a number of times before holding me perfectly still and I felt him pumping his sweet spunk down my throat.

Tucker roared as he blew his load, sounding so much like a wounded animal I hoped the cells were sound-proofed. "Fuck, boy," he said in the throes of after-glow, "You'll be one popular addition to the stud farm."

"What stud farm, sir?" I asked, knowing he'd let on more than he'd meant to.

He recovered quickly. "I meant you'd be an asset to any stud farm, boy. You suck great. I'm sure the deputy will agree." Tucker zipped up and made his way back to the office, leaving my cell unlocked. A few minutes later, Forbes came in, his trousers tenting in a most obvious fashion. I was still on my knees and he marched right up to me, unzipping as he approached. He had his cock out as he said, "Sheriff tells me you're one of the best he's ever had suck his cock. I'm not a skeptical man, but let's feel the proof."

I opened my mouth and he slipped his dick all the way into my gullet. It was long but thinner than Tucker's. "Holy shit," he squealed as I took him right down to his wiry pubes. "The sheriff weren't kidding. Fuck, you got a mouth on you like velvet."

It didn't take me long to get Forbes all sexed up so he dumped a nice load in my gullet. But I wanted more. I had an idea. "I sure am glad," I whined, "that the sheriff didn't want to poke that big ole cock of his in my cherry boy cunt. It would have split me in half." If any of my friends could have heard me right at that moment they would have pissed themselves.

Forbes squeezed my ass. "Sheriff does love him some fine cherry boy ass."

"Oh, please Deputy Forbes. Don't tell him about my sweet ass. I wouldn't be able to sit down for a month if he slammed that monster of his into my tight warm little pussy hole."

You get the idea. I wanted cock in my rear and I was setting it up.

"Well," Forbes said. "It sure would be a sight watching the sheriff bury his porker in your cherry pie."

If that was his idea of dirty talk I was hoping he'd shut up pretty quick smart.

He zipped up and headed for the door. It didn't take the deputy long to pass on what I'd said because Tucker came barreling through the door, his trousers already slipping in his eagerness to get at my butt.

"Assume the position, boy."

I stood and leaned my hands down onto the bed so my ass was invitingly open. I knew Tucker wouldn't be a considerate lover but I didn't care. I needed a good hard fuck and I hoped the spooge already in my ass was all the lubrication I'd need. I heard him spit so I assumed he was at least greasing his prick with saliva. Sure, initial penetration would sting but what's a fuck without a bit of preliminary pain? I like to know I'm being fucked.

I felt him pull my cheeks apart in order to rub the head of his cock up and down over my hole, wanting to tell him to get on with it but I had to get back into character. I whimpered and pleaded for my chastity which just turned him on all the more. "This may hurt a little," he chuckled as I felt him push against my anal sphincter. "In fact, I can guarantee it will hurt like buggery." He laughed at his own joke. He pushed hard and, to his surprise, he slid right in. "What the…?"

I screamed as if he'd split me in half. Forbes came racing to the door. "Shit, I thought you'd killed him."

"Musta pushed into his ass harder than I thought. Slipped right in. His ass is fuckin' tight. Mm, love those virgin assholes."

I wanted to back up on him; demand he fuck me harder. Maybe I could do that with the deputy if he was going to have a go.

Forbes stood watching, holding the interconnecting door open with his body as Tucker rammed into my guts, his cock getting places lesser men never touched. "Hey, sheriff, he's turned on. His cock's hard."

Tucker was triumphant. "The trick is positioning your cock just right as you fuck his ass. It rubs across something called the pros…I don't know why I'm telling you this shit. I don't care if he's getting off on it. I much prefer he didn't. Maybe if he knew what was coming later."

"I thought you were gonna release me," I complained.

"You know what thought did, boy. We got plans for you. You'll bring a pretty penny once we break you in."

I began to struggle as if I was pissed off about his betrayal but it merely made it all the more exciting for me.

I wondered if this is what had happened to Picton and Danzer; whether they had given their asses up to the sheriff and his deputy. They'd never live it down if they had. And what about the Tyson kid? And all the others before him?

It was time to move this investigation to the next level. I squeezed my ass muscles around Tucker's cock, thrusting my body back to engulf it all. I wanted a bit of pleasure from this as well. "Holy fuck, he's milking my prick," the sheriff called to his deputy. "You gotta get a taste of this ass. Best ever. I'll be fuckin' sorry to sell this one." Forbes wandered over for a closer look.

I used every anal skill at my disposal and within minutes Tucker was huffing and puffing. He was either in danger of an imminent heart attack or else he was about to flood my guts with his spunk. While I thought he thoroughly deserved the first, for purely selfish reasons I hoped it was the second. Forbes was already shucking down his trousers in expectation of a go when Tucker bellowed again and thrust awkwardly three or four times, obviously emptying his balls up my ass joining his spooge with the countless deposits that had already been made. Perspiration dripped onto my back when he slumped against me to get his breath. Then, without so much as a thanks or a pat on the ass for a job well done, he pulled out, yanked up his pants, and headed back into the office. "Make it quick deputy. I'm gonna ring the club and tell 'em we have a special delivery."

Forbes moved in behind me and shoved his prick into the spunk custard in my bowels. I flexed for him and he rewarded me with a satisfied grunt. He must have taken the sheriff at his word because he fucked like he was running for a bus. It wasn't exactly unpleasant but I was hoping for a little more finesse. Still, he was hitting all the right spots. "Fuck me harder," I whispered. "Make me feel it. Pinch my nipples."

I don't know whether my request surprised him but he seemed happy to oblige. Reaching around with one hand – the other was holding me steady – he tweaked one nipple and then the other. "Harder," I hissed. This time I gasped with the pain but it had the desired result and my cock leaked. He picked up pace, pushing my head down onto the cell bed so he had better leverage into my ass. Grabbing my waist, he pounded me until I thought he'd ream me a new asshole. My spunk shot out of my cock and landed on the filthy blanket on the bed, my ass muscles gripping the deputy's dick, milking it until he grunted as he shot a load inside me.

"Wowee," he said quietly as he stood still to recover his breath. "That's some ass you've got on you."

Just then Tucker bellowed instructions to bring me into the office where I was handcuffed again before being led outside to the parking lot. I noticed there were no security cameras in the vicinity where their car was parked. I guessed there was no paperwork about my so-called arrest either.

"Where are you taking me?" I simpered as they pushed me onto the back seat of the cop car.

Neither Tucker nor Forbes bothered to respond. I half-heartedly tried a few more questions that I thought someone in my position might ask but all I got in return was silence. I relaxed and enjoyed the view on what turned out to be a half-hour ride to the city limits. There was nothing much on this part of the highway except for a multi-purpose gas station/truck stop/diner. A few rigs dotted the car park, the drivers inside the diner flirting with the big-titted waitress behind the counter which we could see through the plate-glass window.

Tucker didn't pull over, instead heading behind the truck stop where a squat black building stood shielded from the roadway. A dim fluorescent sign that read Damnation Club: Members Only adorned the front. The club appeared rundown and deserted although as soon as the sheriff pulled up, a burly bruiser of a man who I took for security came out to greet us. He was all in black so blended perfectly with the color of the building. He handed Tucker an envelope which the sheriff opened. I caught a glimpse of large denomination bank notes. "Thanks," Tucker grunted and the security guard opened the back door of the police car and dragged me out. "Hey, watch the merchandise," I complained.

As soon as my cuffs had been removed and the key handed back to Forbes, the cops took off. Before I could make a run for it (not that I was going to but security would have expected it) I was hoisted over his shoulder and carried toward the front door of the club. It buzzed open as he approached and he carried me inside.

The exterior was deceptive because the interior was anything but ramshackle. The entrance foyer was luxury itself, a number of doorways leading off to what were labeled Dressing Rooms, Men's Room, Costume Hire, Gym, Office, and the largest which said simply, Dungeon. That was the door security took me through, narrowly avoiding giving me concussion as my head just missed being slammed against the side.

The dungeon seemed to be pitch black until my eyes adjusted. Security shucked me onto a vinyl seat and told me to 'Stay' as if I was some sort of pet. He disappeared through a side entrance giving me time to survey my surroundings. The booths were constructed for privacy but all had a perfect view of the elevated stage at the front of the large warehouse-style room. There were also alcoves around the walls which contained a St. George Cross, slings, or else large metal rings just above man height embedded in the walls. There was also a chain that ran the length of the wall about the level of a man raising his arms above his head.

In the center was a large transparent bathtub that could have easily housed five or six men. Ominously, there was a large drain nearby, small rivulets carved into the painted concrete floor from the alcoves. Around all four walls of the dungeon was a walkway about six or seven meters from the ground. At the back, a small glint of light reflected from what could possibly have been a mirror although I guessed it was probably two-way with the main office behind it in order to watch the activity below.

My reconnaissance was interrupted when the security guard came back into the room. "Boss says to welcome you to the Damnation Club. Hopes you enjoy your stay here. Sorry he can't welcome you in person but he's busy with preparation for next weekend's auction. Said for me to take you to your room." He chuckled on the word 'room.' "Follow me."

He took me through a side door that was hidden from view by a black curtain. The corridor was of stone, miserable with cold and damp. He stopped in front of a heavy wooden door with a barred window and a slot for serving meals. So, I was in a prison of sorts. "It's a full house at the moment," security said. "The boss hopes you don't mind sharing." He swung the door open and pushed me inside. I stumbled, falling heavily. Remaining where I was in order to scope out my surroundings, I was surprised when someone squatted beside me. He put his hand over my mouth to stop me from speaking, then leaned into my ear to whisper, "The place is bugged, be careful what you say."

I recognized the voice. It was Danzer. I nodded that I understood.

Then in a normal voice, he said, "Let me help you up. Are you hurt?"

"Sore ass, bruised ego. That sort of thing. Where the hell are we?"

"Hell. That's the right word for it. We're in the bowels of the Damnation Club."

"Which is what exactly?"

"It's a fetish club for the leather and SM crowd."

"Gay?"

"Exclusively."

I introduced myself. "Vic Tulsa."

"Jack Danzer."

Danzer led me to a corner of the room where we sat on the stone floor away from the uncomfortable looking beds. I assumed he'd swept the cell for bugs and considered this the best spot to converse. Over the next few hours I pieced together the story from his whispered asides in between our normal level conversation, and from his mimed answers.

There were nine of us in all spread out through six cells. Picton was in a cell on his own farther down the corridor. The sheriff had been waiting for the two of them when they hit town, whisking them away before they'd even registered at the local hotel where they had a booking. To all intents and purposes they'd never arrived. Meant someone at the Bureau had a big mouth. Tucker knew they were FBI and was inclined to make an example of them and dump their bodies where they'd never be found but swift talking and the prospect of extra cash from the Damnation Club for genuine FBI agents meant they were sent here.

The inmates were pimped out to anyone who visited the club at night and who had the necessary cash. There was a slave auction scheduled about once a quarter, those who were sold taken away to God only knows where. The next auction was the forthcoming weekend and Danzer expected he and Picton would be sold off or given away because it was too dangerous to have them hanging around. Reluctant to talk about the humiliation he and Picton had endured, all he confided was, "Christ, I don't know how you gay guys get any enjoyment having a cock shoved up your butt." That told me all I needed to know about what had happened to him. He intimated, however, that Picton was finding the entire situation considerably more arousing.

It seems I was never likely to meet the operation's Mr. Big as he was a shadowy figure who never appeared in the club itself, preferring the anonymity of his office overlooking the action. Even Danzer had never seen him or her. Maybe he, or she, was simply a voyeur. I doubted it. More likely a money-hungry sadist.

We were served a pretty good meal after I'd been in custody for a few hours and, having completed it, the cells were opened and we were herded to a communal shower. Although the other guys were very definitely to my liking, we were watched over by a guard who had instructions, so I was told, to prohibit any extra-curricular activity amongst the inmates. All that energy and semen was to be saved for the benefit of paying customers. I did, however, get the opportunity for a few whispered words with Picton who looked as if he was standing up to the pressure remarkably well. Better than Danzer, at any rate. I also clocked the Bridgewood boy who had a belligerent air about him – he was unlikely to be cowered easily. I learned later he was a loudmouth who loved nothing better than baiting the security personnel and the customers and was regularly beaten in the club for his troubles, often crucified on the St. George Cross. I let him be. I didn't think a message that I'd been sent to find him by his father would have put me in his good books. Besides, I didn't need the distraction.

I was told to remain in the shadows that night to watch as the boys fanned out like expensive whores to entice the paying customers into purchasing expensive watered down drinks or else hiring a private room. If you had a tendency toward exhibitionism then, after you'd paid for your companion, you could take him to the sling or the cross or the watersports tub, wherever, and do whatever you wanted in full view of the other patrons. The only club rule prohibited injury or permanent scarring. As I watched, I thought animals in most western zoos were treated better.

Picton seemed popular. At one stage I noticed he was on his knees under a booth table sucking the cocks of a number of wealthy-looking businessmen. He didn't appear too phased by the activity. Danzer and Bridgewood, on the other hand, had a fine line in non-compliance, probably hoping to warn off any potential customers. It didn't work, of course, some men finding their attitude an aphrodisiac or else something they thought they could tame with a riding crop or domination.

Young Bridgewood was attempting to ward of the attentions of a large hairy slug of a man who was attempting to play with his ass, whispering in his ear while pointing to the sling with the encouragement of his buddies who were egging him on. The slug's clothing and body shape screamed conspicuous consumption. There was nothing subtle about him at all. New money, I thought. From the looks of his body, he was probably in IT, spending all his time in front of computers eating crisps and guzzling soda. Could only get his jollies by paying for it, big noting himself in front of his fellow nerds. I looked them over. None of them was anything special but with a bit of a makeover they'd be passable. The slug, though, had no quality that was appealing. Especially not to Tyson Bridgewood, who seemed on the verge of striking him. Up until then I'd been content to lurk in a booth at the back of the club to watch what went on. Weeknights were not especially busy, customers mainly traveling salesmen, truckers, or drug pushers. This night was no exception with a little over two dozen men in solos and various groups dotted around the establishment.

Before things could get out of hand, I strode across to where Bridgewood was about to lose it. I pushed between the two men, facing the slug, smiling my brightest cock-sucking smile. I palmed his erection which, I'm pleased to say, was substantial, then leaned in to kiss him full on the mouth. That startled him but as soon as he heard his buddies yahooing in the background he grabbed me in a death hug to shove his tongue down my throat and his swollen cock against my own. Yeah, I was hard too. I signaled with my free hand for Tyson to fuck off out of there. I had to assume he took my advice because when I came up for air, he was gone. Slug didn't seem to miss him.

"You wanna go over to the sling so me and my buddies can fuck the shit outa your sweet ass."

"Not sure I can take a mancock as big as yours," I said coyly, playing up to his ego. "But I'd sure like to die trying."

He laughed. One of the wandering cashiers made his way over to our little group and after a whispered conversation during which slug looked at me and said, "This is your first night and I'm your very first customer?" to which I nodded my head, money changed hands. When slug obviously said his buddies were also in on the act, further cash was exchanged.

A number of the boys, as well as clients, were watching us and I saw interest in more than a few eyes. Pity I'd never see any of the cash, I needed a new flat-screen TV and my dishwasher was on the fritz.

The deal done, slug, whose name turned out to be Kelly, put his sweaty arm around my shoulder to escort me toward the sling. I counted my admirers. Five in all. I should have me some fun as long as they were half-way experienced and weren't too drunk already. Kelly helped divest me of my shorts and T-shirt – I'd not been fitted out for the club's revealing uniform as yet – so that I was fully naked as he helped me into the sling. I got myself comfortable. One of Kelly's followers restrained my wrists in the padded handcuffs and my legs were hoisted into similar ankle cuffs so that my ass was vulnerable. Kelly tested the sling for height. It was just right. He slid his pants down but kept his business shirt on. By dropping my head back, he could slide his cock into my mouth so I could get it nice and slick for my ass. I didn't want him to do me dry and damage my mancunt. I was pleased to discover there were lube dispensers bolted to the wall and that after I'd sucked Kelly to full erection, he liberally slathered the grease over his cock while one of his minions lubed my hole.

Kelly was a big boy. I felt every inch of his prick slide into me, marking off the inches in my mind until all nine were wedged tightly in my butt. He paused a moment but I wanted the burn to last so I flexed my sphincter to tell him it was okay. "Fuck me, sir," I begged.

He speared into me unexpectedly, the force knocking the breath out of me, making me see stars, but also making my ass feel real good. I pulled his hands down onto my chest, hinting he should play with my nipples. He tugged at them, pinching and twisting so that my ass writhed against his cock and balls. His buddies stood watching for a while, obviously feeling left out because one of them pulled my head back to push his cock into my mouth. It was an average length and thickness so I had no difficulty handling him, giving him a special thrill by swallowing when he was lodged in my throat. That takes real skill.

He didn't last long after that, shooting his wad into me until I swallowed it all down. "Holy fuck," he panted.

That must have been some sort of recommendation because another of Kelly's buddies stepped up to the plate to slide his sizable sausage into my gaping mouth, while

Kelly continued to pound away at my butt. I was hard as fuck in cock heaven. These guys were not the greatest looking or the buffest bodies but they had the one essential ingredient for my enjoyment: they were hungry for my body. It was a match made in gay heaven.

My ass was giving Kelly extra special treatment because his cock was filling me like no other cock had since…well, the last one. My throat was raw as each of his buddies took turns feeding me their spunk as Kelly seemed reluctant to give up my butthole. I encouraged him with a stream of dirty talk that had others within earshot in the club adjusting their crotch, but still Kelly kept pounding, until I thought I'd need a sphincter retread. Finally, he let out a little peep, shoved his cock in as far as it would reach, and shuddered. I felt him flood my guts with his spooge and I shot my bolt as well.

My ordeal was far from over. Kelly thanked me (that was a first) saying, "No one has ever been able to take me for so long without griping. Thanks, man. I'll be sure to hire you again. Even bid for you as my personal slave if the price doesn't go too high." While I enjoyed my moment with the big IT guy, I didn't fancy spending the remainder of my life with him. I was about to explain I wasn't really slave material when my mouth was shut by the insertion of a hard and horny cock that proceeded to fuck my face into near paralysis while another invaded my ass. By the end of the group's paid time, I'd taken enough loads at both ends that I felt like a human blancmange.

A security guard came over to inform them their time was up. Kelly patted my ass as he and his buddies headed to the bar. I was released from the sling and escorted to the showers. It seemed such a pity to waste all that good spooge.

Back on the floor refreshed, I spent the remainder of the night watching the activity. The sex seemed all pretty lackluster and meaningless, but the Damnation Club had to be a goldmine for the owners, especially as the men were all kidnap victims, albeit some of them moving about like sex zombies. It was only later I discovered the 'lifeless' boys were the most feisty and physically aggressive who'd been tranquilized with various drugs. I was surprised Danzer hadn't met the same fate.

The next few nights I joined the other young men in the club, hawking my ass for peanuts and pleasure. I was popular, not least because I was a new (handsome) face. My ass was in constant use to the extent Danzer thought I was enjoying myself a little too much and asked that I be assigned a different cell mate. Fortuitously enough, they put me in the cell with Picton, Danzer's partner. "I know what he says about me," Picton said when we moved to the quiet corner. "I don't know how we can go back to working as partners when this is all over."

At least he was thinking positive, that he had a future back in the real world; most of the other captives believed it would be over for them when they were sold as sex slaves the coming weekend. They really had little concept of what was in store for them; some very rugged patrons let it be known they'd be there to pick up a new slave. Danzer kept up the inquisition about my plans but I couldn't take the chance of being overheard. The Bureau wanted the big guys with the money who had probably bought sex slaves in the past. They wanted to round up as many of the big spenders as they could. The FBI thought they'd be able to wrap up a number of high profile missing persons cases with the help of club members.

Meanwhile, I wanted to get what I could from my term of imprisonment. I'm not boasting when I say I was in no danger of having my asshole close up on me as it got regular workouts each and every night, especially Friday which was the last opportunity for men to test drive the guys they would be bidding on the following evening. I had an army of admirers who I managed to satisfy with just a few thirty-minute breaks every now and then for recovery.

Saturday dawned early for us prisoners. We were fed a protein-heavy breakfast, after which we were pampered with manicures, pedicures, Brazilians, and haircuts. It was drummed into us that as representatives of the Damnation Club, we had to be at our best. I think someone may have forgotten to tell the rah-rah crowd that we were prisoners and unpaid sex slaves. A few of the group were quite buzzy with anticipation while others, including Danzer and young Bridgewood, were fearful or angry. I could use that to our advantage later.

Management was wily enough to keep us separated generally as a group so there was no possibility of hatching a communal plan of escape or disruption. On the very few group occasions we were together, security guards ensured we weren't planning a revolution. I was ostracized by the others who considered me a management spy because of my obvious enjoyment of the sex acts we were expected to perform. Truth is, I did enjoy it, but I am a gay sex addict. I could imagine it was hell for the straight guys in the group.

That day, we were allowed to mix more freely than usual, probably because the powers-that-be couldn't see anyone fomenting a break-out in the short time we'd be together. Sure as hell, I was going to try but it was like pushing shit uphill to get the more skeptical members of the group onside. It wasn't until Danzer snapped, hissing at them, "For fuck's sake, listen to the man. He's an FBI agent sent here to rescue us," that I got co-operation.

The looks of amazement on some faces said it all, however An FBI agent *and* a fag? That would keep. I just hoped a member of the club hadn't overheard the conversation. "Look guys, play it cool this evening. Watch Danzer and Picton and Bridgewood for your cues. Don't concentrate on what I'm doing, pay attention to them. When they start, all hell will break loose and you can play your part. Follow their lead. Just don't let anyone provoke you too early. It could ruin everything."

It was a big ask, given the way we were treated. When the club opened we were dressed in the skimpiest of leather gear, usually a cup hiding out genitals, and either a collar or harness to accentuate our assets, after all, the club wanted maximum return on their 'investment.' Being a comparatively new boy, I'd been there only five days, there was a lot of interest in me. I was touched up, pinched, squeezed, kissed, licked, bitten, and fingered. I loved it, but I guess none of the others did. Even Picton looked distressed at the manhandling.

We were groped by some of the biggest names in the country. I recognized most of them from their pictures in newspapers or on the net. I knew Danzer and Picton and Bridgewood were also committing to memory not only the indignities heaped upon them but also the identities of those who did it. There were men from big business, banking, investments, industry, armaments, and Hollywood big shots including an A-List actor whose hetero exploits were weekly fodder for women's magazines. They brought their entourages with them but, apart from a nod of greeting now and then, the cream of the country's wealth kept very much to themselves and their own group.

Some of the prisoners were looking decidedly jumpy. I hoped they wouldn't give the game away. If we went too early, we may all end up dead.

I threw myself into my role as the center of attention. Sure, I loved all those straining cocks tenting in tight trousers but being an exhibitionist, especially for a group of men who smelled of money and power, both powerful aphrodisiacs, really yanked my chain. Not that my libido ever required assistance.

There was a lot more ass slapping, painful nipple tweaking, and force than on the previous nights. Orders were snapped as if we were trained dogs. In fact, one middle-aged industrialist's entourage consisted entirely of men in doggy hoods and leather body suits with paws and knee pads crawling about the floor. Their cocktails were served in silver dog bowls. That particular patron seemed to have a fondness for Picton, stroking his hair as he squatted between his feet. I imagined Picton kneeling at my feet, lapping between my toes, making… the sting of a riding crop against my ass brought me back to reality.

"You like that?" Mr. Hollywood Actor asked after I'd flinched.

"Yes, sir," I replied, without adding, "Under the right circumstances, but this ain't them."

He ran his hands over my ass cheeks, dipping his finger into my already lubed hole, searching for my prostate. I wondered what the women's mags would say if they had photographs of Mr. Action Hero kissing my abs, finger fucking my ass. It was no concern of mine. I had more immediate problems, like trying to stop from coming every time his finger hit my internal happy button.

I eventually escaped into Kelly's arms. At least he treated me with a modicum of respect although he did thrust his swollen fingers into my ass. I hissed at the pain, but he just kept pushing. As his fingers felt as if they were half-way up my esophagus, one of the security guys interrupted, apologizing profusely telling him there was an urgent phone call on his mobile at the front desk.

All cell phones, computers, anything that could take pictures or broadcast the club's activities were confiscated at the door. If anyone was expecting a call that had to be answered urgently, one of the security personnel would seek them out. I watched Kelly gesticulating wildly as he spoke to his caller; meanwhile his minions were showing their appreciation of my body by rubbing their hands all over it, preparing me for the festive activities later.

I kept an eye on Kelly who now seemed to be seething with anger or frustration. He jabbed a finger at the phone obviously disconnecting the call. He then spoke to security, pointing at me. Security nodded before taking him to the door that led to the office upstairs. He wasn't gone long. He looked like thunder when he returned. "I gotta go, Vic. Meltdown at one of the plants where I'm responsible for IT. Seems some idiot has buggered up the whole system. Don't worry, though, I put in a bid with management. Paid a deposit to show it's in good faith. I'll be coming back for that delectable ass of yours."

"Any time, buddy."

"Come on, guys," he said to his hangers-on, and they all trooped to the entrance to leave.

I signaled to one of the security nannies that I needed the men's. He escorted me backstage to our down-market ablutions block. Clients, it seems, were fussy about seeing us use their luxury conveniences. Security stood outside the cubicle door while I did my business, waiting to take me back to the melee of the cattle show. As we emerged from the back of the stage I almost slipped on a length of chain that had been left lying about. I smacked my hand against the side stage wall to prevent my fall, injuring my wrist at the same time. I growled with pain, the security guy grabbing my hand to see if I'd done any damage. Classic deflection. Danzer and Picton were watching my movements closely.

I was sent back to work where I mingled socially and sexually for the next hour or so until we slaves were all gathered together and moved behind a curtain that had been drawn across the stage area. A makeshift dressing room had been set up. We were told to strip and wait. We all removed what little clothing we were wearing. One by one we were called forward and disappeared. I hoped everything was going according to plan because the auction sounded as if it was about to begin.

I was the last to be called. When security took me onto the stage area, I was greeted by this big bastard: chest hair that you could plait, a jaw that could cut through steel, and a mouth that looked mean as well as commanding. Not that it mattered, but I couldn't tell if he was handsome or ugly as fuck because his face was enveloped in a black leather hood which had two nasty looking long, thick leather horns protruding from the forehead. The only other things he was wearing were a pair of knee high leather boots, leather arm bands, and a black leather pouch that promised a rather large cock. His body was swarthy, but muscular.

His eyes weren't dead or cruel, so I chanced a joke as he shoved me toward the slaves strung up like a row of beans to a length of chain that ran along the back wall just above man height. "Enjoy your work, do you?" I asked.

There was a flash of amusement in those hungry eyes but he suppressed it. "You won't have such a smart mouth once we get through with you." For emphasis, he plunged a dirty thumb between my teeth. I sucked and nibbled on it, rubbing my teeth gently against the knuckle. "Mm, tasty," I said, "but I usually prefer something a bit bigger." I eyed his crotch as I said it.

"You'll get plenty of those," he chuckled. "More than you ever dreamed of. You'll be begging us to stop."

"Not likely," I boasted.

"If I thought you'd be around long enough afterwards, I'd make a bet with you."

I was feeling frisky even as he attached my wrists to the chain. "Go on, risk it. You've got nothing to lose."

"You're a game one. Usually guys are begging me to let them go."

"I'm not your usual guy," I said.

"Obviously."

"So? We got a bet?"

He stopped to look at me up and down as if I were insane. "Okay." He sounded almost admiring. "I bet you'll be begging for me to stop."

"And if I'm not?"

"Name it."

"Then you give me your ass."

He laughed. "Nobody has ever got there and nobody ever will."

"I will." I brazenly winked at him.

"You are so fucked, fag. There hasn't been a man yet who wasn't whimpering by the time the Damnation Club finished with him."

"Prepare to be surprised."

"You're a cocky little thing, aren't you?"

"I know my strengths." I paused for effect. "And my weaknesses."

"What would they be?"

"What? And give you a head start? Fuck that. I will tell you, though, one of my weaknesses is hot and hairy men…like you."

"I'm pretty partial to smooth-assed twinks who can take a lot of punishment."

"That I can, Damnation Man."

"What did you call me?"

"Damnation Man. I don't know your real name. No, don't tell me. It'd be so uncool if you were called Jason or Nigel." I shuddered at the thought. "Damnation Man suits you."

From what I could see of his face, he appeared impressed with the moniker I'd given him.

He chained me up roughly, probably giving me a taste of what was to come. The position was uncomfortable but I hoped I wouldn't be there long enough to care. An announcement came through the speakers, "Gentlemen, welcome to the Damnation Club and our slave auction. You're all familiar with the rules, at the end of the evening you can take any of your successful bids home with you or you can lodge them here at the club for your exclusive use or to rent them out. So, sit back, enjoy yourselves, and get ready to bid."

They were a staid crowd, no whistling, stomping of feet, or general yahooing. As the curtain parted we were on display in all our glory. The paying customers were secluded in their own booths as the security guards distributed leather cock rings which they would fit to each of us. Each booth was numbered and as that number was called the alpha male or one of his minions came down to the stage to fit one of the slaves with the cock hardener.

Some of the slaves were so intimidated by the exposure their cocks had almost disappeared into their bodies ensuring it was necessary that the man on his knees attempting to fit the cock ring show a little oral expertise to get the hanging slave hard. Many of the alpha males weren't willing to be seen in such a subservient position and sent a stand-in. It must have been quite a sight from the audience as each hanging stud had his hard-on ringed. I was last. I waited for a number to be called but instead, Damnation Man marched over to me. My cock was hard already which meant I wouldn't get to feel his mouth…holy fuck, he went down on me anyway. I watched as my cock disappeared into his craw. I almost blew a load.

He didn't keep up his demonstration of superior oral technique for long, snapping the leather band around my cock and balls in a just-short-of-painful position. He strutted along the line, flicking a riding crop at different men. A few copped it on the ass, others on the abs or chest, the back, the legs…and me – on the balls. It was a light enough tap but I saw stars. Had it been much harder, I probably would have puked.

"Bastard," I hissed at him.

For that, I was swatted on the ass, the chain above rattling as I twisted in an attempt to escape the second and third blows. Now there were mutters of approval from the audience.

An impeccably-dressed gent in his forties came down onto the stage, a radio mike in his hand. The auction was officially about to begin. It was conducted in almost total silence from the audience, only the auctioneer's voice disturbing the quiet. The men in the booths merely held aloft a paddle with their number if they were bidding, obviously in pre-arranged increments.

One by one the men were all sold, uncoupled from the overhead chain and taken to their respective new owner. Again, I was the last.

"Now, gentlemen," the auctioneer said. "Just before we get to the final item on tonight's menu, we have a treat. Our resident Master will oblige us with a demonstration of obedience training." He left the stage, leaving me wondering just what this training involved.

I didn't have to wait long. I heard the whistle before I felt the slap of the riding crop across my ass. It stung. Just like the next few swats that turned my butt cheek hot as mustard. Damnation Man alternated the timing as well as my cheeks so I wasn't quite sure when the next blow would fall or where.

What I hadn't anticipated was him turning his attention to my nipples which he struck with a glancing blow of the crop tip. "Shit," I groaned, the pain going straight to my cock. He flicked both of them, again alternating to throw me off balance. I'd never felt anything so painful but at the same time so pleasurable in my life. A couple of swats against my abs and my thighs were small beer in comparison.

He next came at me with a cat o'nine tails, flicking it gently against my body as he didn't want to mark me too heavily before the sale. The strips of leather snaked around my torso leaving red stripes and just enough pain to be worthwhile. My ass also copped a beating before he turned his attention to my blood engorged cock. He struck my erection with such force I thought he'd tear my cock off. His wrist movements were a work of art even as the leather strips wrapped my cock in a blanket of exquisite pain.

"If you don't stop, I'm gonna blow a load," I moaned.

"You begging me to stop?" he asked.

"No, sir. Just warning you."

He struck again before all the words were out of my mouth. I grunted loudly as the cum shot out of my cock in one of the most intense orgasms of my life. When I was emptied of all my spunk, I slumped, supported only by my manacled wrists.

Damnation Man unlocked me and I sank to my knees in the most subservient position I'd ever adopted, my head lowered in exhaustion. He tapped the top of my head with the crop, instructing me to look up. I'm not generally into the domination kick, but for this man I'd be willing to learn. I wanted to feel his body lying on top of me, fucking me into submission. I wanted his cock in my mouth, drowning me with his manly spunk. I wanted…

"This is the FBI, you're all under arrest." It was Danzer, standing on one of the tables.

Fuck, not now. I was just getting started.

There was another shout, Bridgewood this time, then another from Picton. The others got the idea and joined in, creating a cacophony, throwing the audience into confusion. I watched as the slaves revolted. I was their Spartacus. I stood and joined the chorus and the audience rose and rushed to the front door. I felt battered and bruised but proud of what we were doing. Fights broke out as Danzer and Picton attempted to prevent people leaving. Even the security guards couldn't control the situation.

I went to grab Damnation Man, but he'd disappeared. No use going after him, he must have hightailed it out the back. I just hoped the Bureau caught him. He owed me one.

The crush at the front entrance was pushed back as a flank of Bureau agents burst in although they couldn't prevent a few people from escaping. The cavalry had arrived. They battered down the door to the stairs and I soon heard activity in the office behind the two-way mirror and a lot of cursing which meant the person or persons responsible for the club had fled at the first sign of trouble.

Making a triumphant entrance behind the common herd of FBI agents was Bluto Sanchez, no doubt preening for promotion, ready to take credit for the entire operation. Kelly was with him, carrying a number of blankets to wrap the naked slaves who seemed grateful to cover their humiliation.

Sanchez made a bee-line for me. I expected it so I stood naked in defiance, surprised when he said, "Good job, Tulsa. I'm impressed."

Kelly came down with a blanket, wrapping it around my shoulders to protect my (lack of) modesty. "Thanks, Kelly, I owe you."

"Nah." he chuckled. "Just getting my dick in your ass was the greatest thing that's ever happened to me. Wish it was a permanent arrangement."

"So do I, Kelly, but I don't do monogamy. But maybe some lonely Saturday night."

Kelly wandered off happily.

"You let that overweight fuck into your ass?" Sanchez said, obviously disgusted.

"It was part of the job. Besides he's got a great cock. And if it hadn't been for him setting up the small transmitters in the club and shoving that final one up my ass so I could put it on the stage aimed at the audience, you wouldn't have had proof of what goes on here."

"You could have hand-picked someone with a bit more muscle," Sanchez said.

"Like you?" I asked. "Nah, I needed someone with muscle up top where it counts. You may have the body, Sanchez, but for that I needed someone who could successfully pretend to be an IT expert convincingly. You just look like a cop. And Kelly fitted the bill perfectly. Plus I now have an IT guy at my disposal."

"You lucked out there. How'd you recruit him?"

"First night at the club. He was the only one who looked vulnerable. I had to take the chance. While I was up close and personal, I was whispering in his ears. Told him to contact Hass, give the password, and get all of us the fuck out of here."

"What did you offer him?"

"Unlimited free access to my ass."

Sanchez laughed. "Still, you took a chance."

I shrugged. "It paid off. What about the big boss of the operations?"

"No sign of him."

"I think he was tipped off. Same as Tucker was when Danzer and Picton came through the town. By the way, what happened to Tucker?"

"Gone. Packed up and disappeared."

"Yeah, that confirms my suspicions."

"You think we've got at mole at HQ?"

"Looks that way."

Sanchez whistled. "Wouldn't like to be in your shoes when you tell Hass you're accusing one of your co-workers of being corrupt."

"Who says I'm going to tell him. Without proof, it's pointless."

Sanchez surveyed the club. "You know none of this will ever come out in public. They'll all do deals, some of the missing kids will be found, others will still remain in the stats as missing or dead."

"Yeah. But it's one in the eye for Senator Bridgewood, though I don't think there's much love lost between father and son. Not likely to be patched up any time soon, especially when the Senator finds out what Tyson's been through."

Sanchez swatted me on the ass. I must have grimaced. "You're okay for a fag."

I smiled.

"What are you thinking about now?" Sanchez enquired.

"Just remembering Damnation Man."

Sanchez was curious. "Damnation man?"

I grabbed Sanchez's crotch and squeezed. "Nice leather pouch you're wearing tonight, Sanchez. I like it. And the boots. You must have needed them to sprint from the stage to the dressing room to change back into your street clothes and then to the front of the club to make it look as if you were arriving with the other agents. By the way, when are you gonna pay up on our bet. I think I won your ass."

NEW JOCK IN TOWN

They say jocks are dumb. Okay, it might be true for some, but it sure ain't true for yours truly. I'm not talking about exam results or essay marks 'cause I'm pretty mediocre as far as book learnin' is concerned. What I am good at is team sports, especially football, although I'm an all-rounder and I'm super fast and super skilled on the basketball court, and able to hold my own in a pro boxing match; that's what got me my scholarship to Goliath U.

I'd breezed through the first two years of my Communications Degree which will get me sweet fuck all at the end apart from a few impressive looking letters after my name which, so my dad says, will open doors to middle management in the sorts of businesses where I can sit on my ass all day and delegate the really difficult work to the drones who toil beneath me. The alternative is selling used cars or furniture to people who look down their noses at workers in the retail industry.

No use talking about getting a job as a pro sportsman. I'm middle rank there as well but I chose my uni well. No one who has any sense wants to spend time at Goliath U. It's in the bottom ten tertiary establishments as far as scholastic achievement is concerned – yeah, I researched my options before I chose it – but has a middle ranking for sports, so I knew it suited me down to the ground. With my limited sporting prowess and my even more limited head for study, I could parade around campus as one of the head cockies based on my good looks, my trim, muscular body, and my very impressive cock. I wasn't at uni to study, I was there to screw and, as cliché would have it, sow my wild oats.

And for two years, I'd managed to live the dream, more through luck than prowess. I'd been a big leg up the ladder of success to the football team so that we were within a few points of the leaders with a strong chance of reaching the finals – a first for the college. I'd managed a few KOs in the ring as well so that I have a trophy for a Third at the State Championships somewhere at the back of my closet gathering dust. But it was scoring in the bedroom that always counted more and they don't give trophies for that. More's the pity because those I would exhibit with pride.

If you laid all the chicks that I'd balled end to end…well, let's just say, the local stadium would have very few empty seats. I dunno what it is about me; my charm, my dazzling smile, my insatiable cock, my ability to give any chick an orgasm no matter how frigid she is. Okay, I'll come out and say it: In the bedroom, I'm an Einstein of Sex.

Now you've got a bit of background info, you'll understand why my dad's email came as a fuckin' blow to the balls. In it he revealed he'd lost his 'lifetime' job at the financial institution where he worked as…who the fuck knows?…the family had had to downsize to make ends meet, mom had left him because she couldn't adjust downwards, she wanted to adjust upwards just like her waist size, so she'd found a better offer with a wealthy older man and was outa there… well, let's cut a long story short. My newly single loser dad was now living in a demountable home in a trailer park, barely making ends meet in a dead-end job stacking shelves.

I'd swanned through my first two years of uni without a care in the world as dad took care of all the bills. His little boy lived the carefree life because he didn't have to work part-time in shit jobs to pay for tuition and text books. More time for fucking, thank you very much. So what if dad didn't have a well-paid job at present. He was resilient, he'd survive. There'd be plenty of positions available for a man with his background.

Wrong. Seems his skills barely qualified him as a shelf stacker at a local supermarket in an area so down in the mouth it was on anti-depressants.

The situation was brought home to me when my cell phone stopped working because he hadn't paid the monthly plan. Then the internet access dried up. Finally, my brain connected to reality. I was in deep shit. One day I received a letter – you remember letters? – in which dad explained how grave the situation was. Mom had milked the bank account for every penny and he was living on welfare and small jobs he picked up around the town. There was no money for my courses the following semester; there was no money for anything including my air fare home. He wanted me back there for support but I had to pay my own way. I guess I owed the dude that much. Besides, I didn't have enough ready cash to eat during the Spring Break let alone spend on the essentials like beer and babes. I managed to scrounge enough for the bus which lobbed me into the town where I grew up around two days later.

I'd never even passed through the area where dad's trailer park was situated and had to ask directions. Strangers looked at me with pity as they gave directions, warning me of the dangers. I was forced to beg for bus fare on the street using my charm and good looks although a couple of gay dudes decided to try it on offering food and accommodation to what they saw as a country hick newly arrived in town. The offer came with the promise of a 'good time' that meant I'd be face down in their bed, my ass elevated over a pillow or two while they pounded my cherry. Nah, I don't dig dudes for relief, although like all jocks I'd received the occasional drunken blow job from a cute fag at a frat party. That's as far as it went.

I made it to dad's new… uh… accommodation unmolested. I couldn't call it a home. It was sparsely furnished with second-hand junk that looked as if it was held together with chewing gum, and felt even worse to sit in. He was as pleased to see me as I was to be there. I got the lecture about pulling my weight in times of crisis, then the self-indulgent tears about losing his job and his future, detouring through mom being the love of his life, to what a treacherous bitch she was until the tears streaked his face and his sobs became hiccups.

I begged fatigue and escaped to the second bedroom which he'd set up for my visit with a bed and a metal contraption on which to hang my clothes. Pity he'd forgotten to buy hangers. Too tired to curse, I flopped into bed and fell asleep.

Next thing I knew I was being shaken out of a deep slumber in which I was dreaming I had my cock buried to the hilt in my girlfriend, Traci. Not that I knew I was dreaming; it seemed so real. So real, in fact, my cock was hard and throbbing from coitus interruptus. I managed to open one eye but the surroundings were unfamiliar. I was in a bed, at least. Alone, damn it. And someone was shaking me persistently by the shoulder. "Wake up, Sam. Wake up."

That was my dad's voice. Oh, shit. I pulled the sheet more tightly around my body hoping he hadn't seen my hard-on, but it was probably too late. My inauspicious life all came back to me.

"Yeah, dad. What is it?"

"I'm heading off to work. I won't be back until late this afternoon, so you'll have to look after the place. I'm expecting a courier sometime today. When he calls, the parcel is in my bedroom on my desk. Just make sure you get a receipt for it. Okay?"

"Sure, dad."

"I'll see you tonight, son. We can finish our man-to-man then. There's gonna be no freeloading this vacation. You gotta get yourself a job and pay your way. See ya."

"Yeah."

I heard the front door close and then tried to get back to my dream about Traci. It was only two days ago that we parted, promising to keep in touch, but already I missed her. Not quite true: I missed her pussy. Perhaps, her tits. I would have missed her ass but she guarded that like it was the Crown Jewels. Her personality I wouldn't miss. She was a cheer leader and, as a result, believed she was God's gift to…well, the world. She was snobby, snide and superior. Still, there was her pussy that could grip a man's cock like…

I heard hammering on the door. Shit! I must have fallen asleep straight after dad left and he must have forgotten his keys. The knocking was impatient. I guess he didn't want to be late for work. Jumping out of bed, I called, "I'm coming. Hold your horses." Wrenching the door open I was confronted not with my dad but with one of those couriers who wear the tightest shorts known to man. And what a man. As a sporting jock I know a mountain of male when I see one and I'd hate to stack up against this fucker on the football oval. He was like two hundred pounds of solid muscle packed into shorts meant to hold half that.

Only when he looked me up and down and smirked, did I realize I was stark naked, my cock still twitching from its dream about Traci.

"You always greet people like that, son?" he laughed.

"I thought you were my dad, forgot his keys." I was just making it worse.

Patrick, or so the tag on his chest identified him, consulted a computer tablet he held in one hand. "I'm here to pick-up a parcel from a Mr. Stan Jackson. Would that be you?"

"That's my dad," I said, cupping my hands unsuccessfully over my genitals. "But if you hold on I'll go get the parcel. Just wait there."

I turned and headed for dad's room, all too aware that Patrick had his eyes glued to my ass, because I heard his sharp intake of breath and a low whistle which he probably hadn't meant me to hear. There was no point attempting to cover up now but I made a detour to the bedroom to grab my shorts before I went to retrieve the parcel that Patrick was here to pick up.

I'd flung my clothes every which way the night before, and as I was bending to see if my shorts were under the bed

I felt a warm hand against my ass cheek. I jumped and screamed like a girl.

"What the fuck!" I turned to face Patrick. He must have followed me inside. I should have closed the door in his fuckin' face and made him wait outside.

"That's some package you got there," he smiled.

"Yeah, well it's not the package you were paid to pick up, so get your hands off it."

Instead of taking any notice of my demand, Patrick pulled me against his body, gripping my ass cheeks, massaging them in his strong hands, his hard cock pressing against my stomach.

WTF! Until that moment I hadn't realized Patrick had shed his courier's uniform and was as naked as I was. Okay, in my aroused state from the dream about Traci it felt good having a hot body against mine, my treacherous cock filling with blood and embarrassing me. My cock didn't care – the prospect of getting some action was all important.

But not this sort of action. The dude tried to kiss me. I felt his cheek, rough as sandpaper, against my face. "Fuck off, dude!" I spat, emphasizing the point by shoving him hard in the chest. My hands hit a wall of solid muscle that failed to move him one inch. "I don't do fag shit."

"Your cock says otherwise." So saying he wrapped his fist around my shaft and began to milk it slowly.

"At my age my cock stays hard almost all the time. Anything sets it off, so don't take it personally when I ask you to take your hand off my privates."

He stilled his hand, looking deep into my eyes until I turned away in case he saw all my secrets. "Don't tell me you never got a blow job from another dude."

I was going to lie but I knew he'd see straight through me. "That's different."

"Different how?"

Why was I even discussing it with him? He was molesting me; I should be fuckin' screaming the place down.

"I was drunk, I didn't care."

Patrick looked around the room. "Where's your dad keep his liquor?"

I couldn't help it; I laughed.

"There, that's better. You're even better looking when you smile."

"Stop with the compliments. I know I look good, I don't need no dude to tell me."

"You must get lots of compliments," he said. "You must be very popular. Good looking, hot bod, huge cock, and an ass that was made to be fucked."

"Piss off," I yelled. "No one touches my ass."

"People have tried?"

"A few. They don't get very far. If they don't back off after I ask them to, then they get a black eye or a split lip."

Patrick put both hands in the air as if in surrender, even though my threat was hollow where he was concerned. He was such a big fucker he could have demolished me with one hand. "Looks like I'll have to settle on just giving you one of my patented spectacular blow jobs."

My cock twitched in anticipation and, truth be known, I was so horny, I was willing to let this muscle hunk chow down on my family jewels. He pushed me back on my bed so that I fell with my legs apart, my cock bobbing in the air like a fat Triffid looking for prey. Patrick hunkered down over my cock, blowing his warm breath against my balls before his tongue flicked out to lather them in his spit. He took each testicle into his mouth, chewed on it gently, forcing my cock to ooze pre-cum. Rubbing his hands across my abs and up to my chest, he squeezed my pecs and pinched my nipples. It was painful but it sent an electrical charge straight to my balls where he was nibbling and sucking. Stroking his nose up my shaft, inhaling my scent, moaning his appreciation, I wanted to grab his head and ram it down on my cock. I needed relief real bad.

"Come on, dude, suck it if you're going to." I sounded whiny even to myself.

"Patience, dude." He repeated 'dude' with an edge of sarcasm that I didn't appreciate. "Do you treat your girlfriend like this?"

"Pretty much," I said proudly. "And if she complains I dump her and get another one who won't."

He sat back on his heels and looked up at me. "You really are a total charmer." Then he shrugged. "What do I care? I don't want to marry you, just suck this hot cock of yours."

As if to prove his point he opened his mouth, licking the slit before he engulfed my hardness in his warm, wet mouth. My body jolted as the pleasure shot through me. This guy was an expert cocksucker. Sure, a few of the chicks I dated were good but this guy knew what turns a man on and his tongue had a life of its own as he bobbed his head against my stomach attempting to stuff as much of my dick down his throat as was humanly possible. I'd had chicks deep throat me but they usually gagged after a few seconds but this dude could do things with his throat muscles without snot running out his nose that made my toes curl.

I grabbed the back of his head and jammed my prick as far down his gob as it would go. When he began to struggle I let him bob up for air. "Take it easy, man," he complained. "I'll get you off. In my own good time. Just relax."

I was horny and I didn't want him taking all day about it. This was about me, after all. "Haven't you got other deliveries to make?"

I should have kept my mouth shut with the questions because he had to take his lips from around my cock to answer, and I did enjoy watching me slide into his face. "And more cocks to suck, but you're new and I want to show you how good I am. Maybe get you addicted to what I can do for you so I can do it again."

"Don't go getting any ideas, dude," I said, although with my lack of cash meaning I wouldn't be able to wine, dine, and dick many chicks, having Patrick on stand-by did have some appeal. "I prefer cunt. And I don't have any trouble getting it."

"Suit yourself," he said before going back to what he did best.

As he sucked and tongued my hardness, he tugged at my balls just this side of pain, interspersing that with rubbing his hands across my abs and up to my chest where he pinched my nipples which just brought me closer to climax. Patrick knew ways to excite my body that none of the babes I dated did, although when he moved his hands to my ass, I let him squeeze my butt cheeks because that felt so good. When he attempted to worm a finger into my crack, I moved his hands away pretty quickly.

He came up for air. "Okay, man. I can take a hint. But you've got such a sweet ass, how about you let me lick your hole. I promise no funny stuff."

Only once had a chick tongued my asshole. She was some slut who'd do anything for dick and because I'd heard so many good things about having your ass rimmed, I thought there was no time like the present to take her up on her offer. Okay, I liked it. It seemed so…decadent. She ate ass like she was starving for it, making me squirm so much I almost blew my load while she had her tongue wedged up there. No one else had ever offered and now that Patrick had planted the idea in my head, I guess it became appealing. Sure, he could go back on his promise but there was nothing stopping him from totally dominating me now.

"Okay," I said.

"Turn over on your stomach and part your legs."

I did as he instructed, feeling the mattress dip as he got behind me, his hands parting my cheeks. I flinched as I felt his breath against my crack. His tongue licked down the crack to my balls, making me shiver in anticipation as he glided across my ass entrance. Then he reversed, his tongue sliding upwards. I wanted nothing better than to grab his head and pull his face against my butt.

His mouth returned to my anus and he licked until it was slick with spit, then he began to push his tongue against the entrance. I clenched, but through a series of sucks, licks and pushes he got me to relax until he got his tongue inside me. I tried not to groan because the feeling was incredible but I didn't want him to know he was getting to me. I relaxed into a sex haze not caring the gender of the person who was playing such amazing sex tunes on my body. My cock dribbled, perilously close to shooting a load, and I wanted to dump in Patrick's throat. "Dude," I murmured, "I can't take any more."

He knew what I meant so he let my cheeks go, pulling his face slick with spit and my ass funk away from my hole, then he urged me onto my back, smiling contentedly before he sank that hot mouth around my cock. I bucked into his mouth forcing it as far down his throat as I could possibly go, not even realizing he'd shoved his middle finger into my ass as I did so. I was too far gone to complain, especially when he found some magic button buried deep inside me and by rubbing his finger over it he released a geyser of cum from my balls that shot straight into his mouth. Damn, that was hot. Reluctantly, I pulled out to allow him to spit my juice onto the sheets or race to the toilet to gargle the taste away. Hell, no, he swallowed every drop and went back to clean up the last-minute oozings from my slit. You've got no idea how rare it is for college chicks to swallow. That's why a lot of guys prefer older or married women.

When he'd finished, I said lazily, "If I wasn't so exhausted by what you just did, I'd get up and slap you around a bit."

"It was only a finger, dude, not a cock. No lasting damage. Besides, you liked it."

"Yeah, that's the problem."

"If it sets your mind at ease, it doesn't mean you're gay. Lots of straight guys like their prostate massaged."

"If you say so." I got up and eased my shorts on; amazed my ass didn't hurt at all. I retrieved the package from dad's bedroom, made sure I got a receipt, and Patrick went to the door. He hesitated a moment. "Hope you don't mind me saying so, but you're something special." He took a card from his wallet. "Give me a ring sometime." I went to object though the memory of that asshole rimming may have got him a return bout. "It's not what you think. I do a few sex toy demonstrations for hen's nights and women's groups. Like a Tupperware Party but with dildos and vibrators. Bit of dick flashing, bit of cunt licking, the occasional fuck or two. Chicks are getting more demanding so it's almost too much for one man. If you want to make a bit of extra cash, give me a call sometime. You look like the sort of guy who'd be up for a bit of fun and games. I'll leave my card."

He put it on the table and headed off whistling. I picked the card up intending to dispose of it in the garbage but filed it in my back pocket instead. I didn't want my dad to find it even though I had no intention of following up, but after two days of my pathetic tosser of a dad nagging me about what a lazy piece of crud had sprung from his loins, I was about to deck the man. In hindsight, I guess I shouldn't have drunk all his beers, the only treat he had those days after he crawled home from his second job as a warehouse inventory clerk. I got the lecture about pulling my weight, and about the tens of thousands of dollars he'd spent on my upbringing.

His ultimatum was to get a job by the end of week – any job – and start paying my way or get the hell out of his house. He punctuated his threat by slamming his bedroom door. Peace at last. I needed to get out of there even if only for a takeaway pizza. Dad's diet consisted almost entirely of noodles and beans and whatever he could afford at the staff canteens where he worked. That wasn't much help to me and if I ate another pot noodle I was in danger of speaking Chinese.

Fortunately, dad had thrown his coat over the back of the chair when he got home, leaving it there when he stormed off to his room. I rifled through the pockets hoping that I'd find if not his wallet then at least some loose change. No such luck. I cursed. My foot nudged something cold that must have fallen out of his pocket when I lifted the coat up. It was a cell phone. The bastard told me he couldn't afford one when I told him I needed to ring Traci.

I keyed in her number, eager to hear her voice. The call was brief and to the point. She didn't sound as if she missed me one bit. There was party noise in the background and she seemed anxious to get back to it. She was pissed off that I hadn't been in touch even though I attempted to explain the situation. She merely yawned in my ear. No, she couldn't help me out with any money so I could join her. I was about to remonstrate with her that we didn't seem to have much of a relationship when she said brusquely, "Gotta go," and disconnected before I could reply. Fuck her.

Scrolling through the numbers dad had programmed into the phone I found one for mom. Nothing ventured…I pressed it.

It was answered almost immediately. "Stan, I told you to stop ringing—"

"Hey, mom," I said.

"Sammy? Is that you?"

"Yeah, mom. I miss you."

"I miss you too, baby. Where are you?"

"I'm at dad's place. Things are bad."

"He'll get over it."

"Not him. Me. I have no money, no prospects."

"Oh, baby. That's simple."

Thank God for moms. She was about to bail me out. I could go live with her until things got back to normal or she could give me some of the cash she'd siphoned out of their joint account. "Glad to hear it because I'm totally broke."

"Baby, don't be so down in the dumps. No one will employ you if you're a miserable bastard."

"I thought—"

"Yeah, I know what you thought, baby. The solution to your problem is easy. Get a job. Just like I've had to do."

I heard her cackle as she disconnected.

Obviously the cell phone was cursed and I was about to fling it across the room so it would smash against the wall. Fortunately, I realized in time dad needed it for work so I slipped it into his coat pocket. There was sweet FA to do as dad didn't have a TV, but it was much too early to go to bed so I grabbed my tablet and headed out to find free Wi-Fi connection at one of the burger or chicken takeaway chain stores so I could at least get in contact with the outside world and check up on my Facebook friends. Way to get even more depressed. Not one of my buddies in the team had bothered to send me any sort of email but they'd had plenty of time to update their status on social media, rubbing my nose in their adventures with surf, sun and sex while I battled suffocation, stasis, and solo masturbation. Life was a real gonad kicker.

I was about to pack up and leave because the staff were eyeing me suspiciously. The joint was practically empty and I hadn't bought even the cheapest item on the menu. I stood up and something fell out of the back pocket of my grungy shorts. I bent down to retrieve it. Fate? The Devil's work? Whatever it was, it was a lifesaver. Patrick's card. Without the necessary coin to ring his cell phone, I could at least contact him via his listed email. There was no point in prevaricating, so I wrote about my predicament in a straightforward way without pulling on his heart strings and without self-pity, explaining that I was broke and I needed a job – any job. I also told him I had no means of communication except via email.

Not expecting he'd be sitting waiting for a message from me, I decided to give him ten minutes to respond, otherwise I'd check again in the morning. I was in luck. He responded from his cell phone that he was in the area and would stop by my dad's place and pick me up. Even though I'm not a fag I would have sucked his dick I was so pleased to see him. He took me out for pizza, then to a bar for a round of beers. I promised I'd pay him back but he dismissed my offer with, "Forget it, it's all a tax deduction." Then he laughed. "That is if I paid tax on my party earnings."

He had a job coming up the following Friday. A hen's night. "They get a bit rowdy," he explained. "They like to see a bit of cock, feel a bit of cock, maybe the bride-to-be likes to suck it a little. I can lap cunt like it's the elixir of life but my dick rarely stays hard for long when it's tits and fanny, so you're the ideal partner. You got any objections to letting a few chicks play with your family jewels?"

"None at all."

"You got any costumes?" He noticed my puzzled look. "Cops, firemen, construction worker? No? I'll pick you up same time tomorrow night and we'll get you kitted out. Oh, just to keep you on stand-by, here's a hundred bucks to help you out till you make real money on Friday." I loved the guy. I loved the guy so much that later in his van I let him chow down on my cock until he got a bellyful of spunk. Seemed a satisfactory exchange rate.

That money kept my dad off my back when I explained it was a small advance on my wages. Of course, I didn't tell him what I was really doing, just that I'd got a job with a catering company and I was a barman/waiter. He sneered until I told him the sort of money I'd be making – I lied, I toned the figure down so I could stash some of it aside for me – but, even so, he whistled in admiration.

Sure as shit, I was nervous on Friday when Patrick drove us out to the burbs. He gave me some last-minute instructions before assuring me I'd be fine. "There's nothing to be nervous about. You take your pill?"

I nodded. I'd taken the cock stiffener an hour before and already I could feel its effects. Every time I glanced at Patrick as he talked me through the night's activities, I watched his lips and imagined them around my dick. I probably didn't need the pill on top of everything else. The prospect of getting me some chick sucking or maybe a bit of pussy had me edging all night.

Patrick pulled into an ordinary suburban street with a MacMansion lit up like a Christmas tree, loud music thumping out a bass beat, the sound of raucous female laughter echoing along the pavement. I've been at football matches with less noise.

We were greeted by a gaggle of around twenty women, most of whom were already three sheets to the wind and who were very touchy feely when we were ushered into the house. The place reeked of alcohol – cans of beer and empty bottles of the hard stuff littered the kitchen – and the chicks were ready to rock. Patrick called for calm and although they quieted for a time I knew what a missionary felt like in the midst of starving cannibals.

They cleared a spot for us to set up. Patrick made money on the side by selling the sex toys he demonstrated. He was an astute businessman and the women didn't know where to look when he opened his box of goodies. That didn't stop them from grabbing at everything demanding to know what it was for until Patrick whistled to call a halt to the melee. "Ladies, if you'd just be patient. Take a seat and we'll show you what each and every one of these delightful items can do to make your pleasure even more pleasurable."

Then it was my turn. I'd learned the script until it sounded natural enough. "It's rather warm tonight so why don't we all make ourselves more comfortable." That was the signal for me to peel off the white T-shirt that highlighted my upper body, to reveal my tanned abs, pecs and biceps. There was a cheer from the crowd and, as rehearsed, Patrick shrugged before shucking off his own

T-shirt. That brought gasps of admiration. He was one buff fucker. We encouraged our audience to 'get comfortable' as well and a few of the drunker or more adventurous removed their tops to let their tits hang free. Only one or two of them stripped right off and the sight of their naked bodies inflamed Little Sammy until he was straining against my black dress pants, obvious to anyone who looked.

We started easy, demonstrating nipple clamps, leather harnesses, and hoods, involving as much audience participation as possible. I made sure to fondle the tits of any woman who wanted to experience first-hand the clamps biting into her nipples, sucking them briefly after I'd removed the painful device. This merely encouraged a few more partygoers to rip off their tops. While Patrick worked one side of the room I worked the side with the two totally naked women. They were very keen on the vibrators, dildos and anal balls.

"I don't seem to be moist enough," one of the women complained as she attempted to insert one of the larger items into her pussy. I looked to Patrick who was busy massaging an overweight woman's breasts after she'd endured her nipples squeezed in a mechanical device. He shrugged. That was good enough.

"Here. Let me help you," I said removing the offending dildo before burying my face in her cunt and proceeding to lap it like a kitten laps milk. She squealed with delight, grinding her pelvis into my face until I thought I might suffocate; her screams as she climaxed were enough to wake the neighborhood. As I came up for air, I noticed a few more women had stripped completely.

Patrick took charge once again. "Well, ladies, that seems to have broken the ice. How about we show you a few items that might help your husband or your boyfriend. Are you ready?"

The women screamed as both Patrick and I gyrated clumsily and ripped off our trousers in one professional movement. Ah, the joys of Velcro. We were naked underneath because we weren't about teasing, we were about selling sex. We got the women to bind our genitals with various cock rings – leather and metal – although both of us were in pain as they were fitted around our erections. Cock rings are best placed when you're limp. A number of women took the opportunity while down on their knees in front of us to put their lips around our cocks for a quick taste. "'Come on, Nikki, come and join the fun," one chick called to a woman who held back from the crowd.

"I can't," Nikki stuttered. "It would be like being unfaithful to Brad."

I guessed Nikki was the bride-to-be.

"What?" another woman said in amazement. "You don't think your precious Brad is off fucking some sleazy stripper at his bachelor party?"

Nikki was indignant. "Of course not. Brad isn't like that."

"Oh, honey," a woman who'd just had a good taste of my dick replied. "All men are like that."

Another added, "My Harry is organizing the bachelor party and I know for a fact, your Brad is as eager as all his buddies to fuck the strippers they've got lined up as entertainment. But you know what? Keep your legs together, Nikki. We all admire you for that. But you'll spend the rest of your life – always assuming you and Brad last that long together – wondering what another man's cock is like."

"This is your opportunity, honey. Go for it."

I could tell Nikki needed a bit of encouragement, so I slithered over to her, caressed her face and began a slow dance with her. Tense at first, she soon relaxed into my rhythm as I cooed sweet nothings in her ear. She wasn't pretty, but she wasn't ugly either, just average. I made her feel important and beautiful and soon she was rubbing herself against my cock, her hands creeping down my back until she had two handfuls of my butt cheeks. I leaned in to kiss her lips. I wasn't aggressive, merely flicking my tongue over her mouth until she sighed and opened up. I kissed her gently and she melted against me.

All eyes in the room were on us, the atmosphere electric, some women now openly fingering their pussy or even helping out one another. I slowly peeled off Nikki's top until her breasts were bare, pinching them softly until they were hard with arousal before pasting my mouth over each in turn, nibbling gently with my teeth before licking and sucking until I had Nikki in my power. I felt the moment she let go totally, surrendering all power to me.

It was just a matter of relieving her of the rest of her clothes as sensually as possible until she stood naked and proud, beaming at my encouragement and compliments. I picked her up to the hoots and cheers of the other women who were now much taken with the strap-on dildo Patrick was showing them. Down the hallway, I found the bedroom, kicking the door closed behind me as I carried Nikki to the bed. She was shivering, with anticipation I expect, as I stripped off the bed cover, before laying her on the sheets. Beside her, I ran my fingers across her breasts and down to her thighs then on to her pussy to push my thumb gently inside her, spreading her open so that I could rub my finger across her clitoris.

Once I had her gasping with desire, I slid down her body until my face was level with her moist pussy. Placing her legs gently on my shoulders, I entered her with my tongue. She was so pliable I had no problem bringing her off the first time merely by licking and tongue fucking her until my mouth was covered with her juice. While she was still relaxed but sensitive, I kneeled up on the bed and aimed my cock at her moist hole. She looked me in the eye. "Go on, do it," she whispered.

I sank inside her, my moan of pleasure equal to hers. It had been ages since my cock had been squeezed by a hot pussy. I rode her slowly, acutely aware this wasn't about my pleasure but hers. After she came a second time, I increased the pace just enough that Nikki would know she was being fucked rather than loved this time. She met my every thrust with enthusiasm until I felt I could no longer hold back, pumping my seed deep inside her, making her scream as she climaxed for the third time. I only hoped her hubby-to-be could achieve the same results or else poor Nikki was gonna be a very disgruntled wife.

Holding her until she went through the various stages of guilt, she sighed at last. "I'll never forget you."

"Me either," I lied. "Your husband is a very lucky man."

I gave her a few more moments before suggesting we go back to the party where we were greeted by so much bawdy good humor Nikki blushed.

I was surprised that the centerpiece of the party was Patrick on his hands and knees, his face buried in one woman's cunt while one of the more adventurous women had donned the strap-on and was right royally riding him. A third lay on her back sucking Patrick's prodigious weapon.

The remainder of the evening unfolded in much the same manner. Although I fucked a few more women, I never took any of them to the bedroom. That had to be Nikki's special moment. My cock was fondled, sucked, pinched in so many different ways by so many different women, I lost track. Patrick licked cunt, allowed his cock to be sucked, even had dildos shoved in his ass, but he never fucked the women. It surprised me that they didn't mind because his cock was huge, bigger even than mine, and had I been a woman, I would definitely have wanted it inside me.

As the party wound down, the partygoers exhausted, some of them spattered with our sperm, my cock was still like a rod of iron. I could have gone on for hours. I'd write a note of thanks to the pharmaceutical companies that had invented various dick hardener pills tomorrow.

"Look, Sammy is still stiff as a board," a woman exclaimed.

"You know," another joined in, "I've always wanted to watch two guys do each other."

There was a frenzy of agreement even as both Patrick and I attempted to dampen down the enthusiasm.

"Go on, Sammy. Fuck Patrick in the ass."

"He can take it. Go on."

The women took up a chant. I wasn't totally turned off by the idea because Patrick's ass was hot and my cock had certainly twitched in appreciation as I caught a brief glimpse of the strap-on stretching his ass cunt. I wasn't sure though how he'd feel about having my big dick buried in his guts. Again with his shrug. Why was he leaving all the decisions to me? Okay, if that's how he wanted to play the game.

"Suck my cock, motherfucker," I ordered.

There was a hush from the room as they watched to see how this would play out. I was as much in the dark as they were.

Patrick hesitated for a second or two before scrambling across the room to kneel at my feet. He looked up into my eyes and winked before putting his mouth around my cock and swallowing it all the way down to my balls in one gulp. There were gasps of amazement from the women watching. "How does he do that?"

"He should give lessons."

"If I could do that to my husband he wouldn't be fucking every stray bimbo that crosses his path."

I felt Patrick snicker around my prick. It was show time. I held the back of his head and fucked his face hard, then backed off to allow him to do all the work. We varied the pace and the rhythm until I felt we'd milked it long enough. After all, I knew his oral technique from the countless times he'd blown me since we first met. I'm no fag but when the pussy isn't available…

"On your back," I ordered.

Patrick complied, stretching his legs to the side so that his ass was wide open. I ordered two women to hold him in that position and they grabbed his ankles. I could see his ass cunt was well lubed from the previous strap-on fucking he'd received. I wiped some of the excess on my cock although Patrick's saliva had slicked me up. Aiming my cock at his hole, I pushed forward. As I entered him, Patrick moaned, and the women surged forward to get a better look.

"Fuck him hard," a woman ordered. "Like I'd want to fuck my boyfriend if I had a cock."

She'd be buying a strap-on before the night was out.

Patrick nodded almost imperceptibly and I picked up the pace until I was slamming into his ass. It was only then that I realized I'd crossed a line. I was fucking another dude's butt. And I was fucking loving it. Patrick's ass was squeezing me every time I pounded inside. His fuck tube was hot as hell and twice as clinging. Oh, man, what had I been missing? Didn't mean I was a fag. This made Patrick a fag, not me.

"Go on, kiss him."

I baulked at that command until I felt a hand on the back of my head and someone behind me pushed my face down onto Patrick's. He seemed to have no qualms and as our lips touched – as far as I intended to go – he opened his mouth, tickling mine with his tongue until I opened up. Fuck, this was faggy. I justified it on the grounds that I was being coerced into it. I attacked his mouth with the same energy I attacked his ass. This was pure sex. I didn't care about the guy under me; I just wanted to get off. I stabbed his mouth with my tongue, the hand on the back of my head long since relinquishing its grip.

Patrick grabbed my butt to pull me deeper inside him, his fingers so pleasurably painful they must have left indents. I was huffing like an old steam train heading closer and closer to the precipice. We'd given up kissing to concentrate on our orgasm when I heard Patrick moan that he was going to come. Good. I was about to blow my load as well. He beat me. With a roar, he shot his load all over his stomach, the grip of his pulsating sphincter drawing my spunk out of my balls, blasting it into his ass.

As I pulled out, I wondered what I'd got myself into.

Patrick showered first, giving me time when it was my turn to wonder whether tonight's activity meant I was a fag. None of it had repulsed me. In fact, I'd enjoyed it. Maybe I was bi. I'd have to think about it later because I had to get back out there and sell.

We made a killing. Apart from sales of the sex apparatus and our appearance fee, the women were very generous tippers. We both received a few phone numbers – Patrick's best from a woman who wanted to watch him fuck her husband – and the promise of repeat business as soon as another of their friends married.

Packed up and comfortable in Patrick's van for the silent ride home, Patrick was the first to speak. "I'm sorry, man. That wasn't intentional."

I knew he was speaking about the fuck. "Nothing to worry about, dude. It was hot."

He almost seemed afraid to ask. "Still friends?"

I attempted to ease his mind in the best manner available. "When the next gig?"

He looked at me strangely. "You serious?"

"Of course, I'm fuckin' serious. There's fifteen hundred bucks in that stash you gave me after that little sex concert. Where else am I gonna make that much money for so little work and so much pleasure?"

"Well, now that you ask…"

I didn't give my dad money the next day; I saved it up to present to him at the end of my first week. I kept most of it for myself, paying him just slightly more than the going rate would be for what I was supposed to be doing: waitering and bar tending. The little extra I gave him I explained away as tips. He got off my case pretty much after my first 'pay packet' and, as I continued to bring in the money every week, his mood perked up and he became almost too friendly. I didn't really need a clingy dad, let alone one as a best friend.

I had Patrick for that. Word of mouth got around and business picked up. We became a popular duo although maybe not up there with Batman and Robin, the two superheroes we sometimes dressed as. That usually led to requests for Robin to do Batman at the end of the party. In fact, it became our signature. I overcame my fag prejudice as well as my reluctance after Patrick showed me a few gay porn videos in which he pointed out straight guys who were gay-for-pay: they did it for the money. I'd never heard of it but it salved my conscience, especially when a few of the straight guys in the movies also kissed their male partners for the pay check. I learned to relax and have fun, and I was soon stashing the money away. I bought a car, nothing ostentatious, but enough to get around. I was fucking pussy on the side although the work kept my cock pretty content.

Things settled into a pattern. In fact, I was making so much dough that at the end of Spring Break I went back to the uni flush with success. I lasted two weeks. I didn't care about the classes or the degree any more. Plus my buddies all seemed so juvenile now. Something had changed in my personality, not least that my dad meant nothing to me. By the time I left his house – it would never be a home to me – I knew I'd never see him again. We'd tried talking but that merely reinforced we had absolutely nothing in common. It was sad, I suppose, but some kids outgrow their parents. We'd never been particularly close, but I did owe him. I left a couple of grand for him while he was at work, plus a note that read "Thanks for everything. See ya."

I felt much the same about university. It was a dead end. After a fortnight, I was ready to bail. I rang Patrick who seemed pleased to hear from me.

"Hey, man, how's the higher education going?"

"It sucks."

"Not as good as me, I bet."

I laughed. The first good laugh I'd had since I'd left. And, if I was honest, his blow jobs were better than any I'd received since I'd been back at uni.

"I was wondering…"

"Yeah, I miss ya. The chicks miss ya even more."

I'm not dumb. I know Patrick missed me because I was the secret of his success. I brought in the money and I'd left him desperately looking for a substitute. He'd been bitter when I told him of my plans to return to uni to further my education. He'd pleaded, he'd begged, he'd threatened, he'd bribed, but in the end I knew I had to do it. I was glad I did otherwise if I'd stayed with Patrick's business I'd be forever wondering if I'd done the right thing. On my return to Patrick's fold, I found myself an apartment as far away from my dad as it was possible to get. Patrick offered to share his place but I wanted my freedom.

We put the unpleasantness of our parting behind us for the sake of our business although I noticed some of the former warmth was missing. Patrick no longer offered to blow me when I was horny and when we exhibition fucked at the parties, his ass might be in it but I could see his mind and his heart weren't.

It all fell into place after one particularly exhausting party at which the participants were stingy in their appreciation. We'd made a lot less than usual. Patrick was in a surly mood. I tried cheering him up, to no avail.

"Why is it you always get to fuck me?" Patrick snapped. "I think it's about time I got my cock in your ass."

I laughed, thinking it was a joke. "Not part of the deal, man."

"Maybe we need to change the deal then."

I tried to keep it light. "Don't think so. You can stick your tongue where the sun don't shine but no way is anyone getting their cock inside me."

"In that case, maybe you shouldn't expect a fifty/fifty cut."

I was about to point out that I did all the cunt fucking but I guess that was offset by the fact he got ass fucked by the strap-on as well as by me. Instead, I asked, "What's got into you, dude?"

"Sorry. Business is tapering off. We're old news. There's just so many people in this rat hole of a town before everybody's been there/seen us. Our profit is flatlining. We have to come up with some new ideas. The formula is tired."

"I guess that makes sense but I'm not crossing that line about my ass."

"We might have to move to a larger town."

I shrugged. "That's okay by me."

I had considered branching out on my own, but I was sensible enough to realize that what sold us was the male-on-male fucking that climaxed the evening. I wasn't prepared to train a substitute for Patrick. Call me lazy, but I was happy to ride along on his planning, expertise, and his hot ass. In fact, I quite looked forward to fucking his tight hole because it was something different from all the pussy I was getting. Pussy was becoming a job. Fucking Patrick's ass was for pleasure.

But things didn't get better; they got worse. The bookings were drying up. Others learned from our success and went one or two better. Patrick, too, was going off the boil. He had a new mate, Warren, a fucker even bigger than Patrick himself in all departments because he was a personal trainer and obviously a professional body builder. His balls were like a bull's and his cock was a size queen's delight. He'd come along on one of our hen's nights when a third had been requested and Warren did the honors. I actually flinched every time his cock buggered Patrick's hole. That was how their relationship began.

I found myself more and more on the outer, particularly after I informed Patrick I wouldn't countenance giving up my ass for the prospect of more cash. We were making almost as much as we were at the height of our success, so I was content. I'm not a greedy bugger, just protective of my anal cherry. I'd long since come to the conclusion I was bisexual and because I worked with people for whom that was no big deal, I'd been spared a lot of denial and soul searching.

I don't know what made me doubt Patrick was paying me what I was worth. Perhaps it was the way he hurriedly divvied the spoils at the end of the night, stuffing his share in the glove box of his van after presenting me with mine, but I decided to investigate. One night, after a really grueling session in which none of the women seemed pleased with anything we did, Patrick handed me my share which was around the usual amount and placed his in the usual spot. I was slow to get out of his van as he stormed off in a huff once he'd reached home – and Warren who was waiting for him – where I usually picked up my own car to drive to my apartment. I quickly opened the glove box and counted out his cash. I was right, there was a big difference in our payments, but in the totally wrong way.

Patrick was subsidizing my cut by taking less himself. Just to make sure, I repeated the subterfuge over the next few parties. It was true. Shit. I felt low. He'd talked about getting out of the business because he and Warren wanted to move, set up a business somewhere. They had dreams of opening a gym in LA to cater for all the muscle studs and film stars. I thought it was probably a much over-catered market. But, hell, it was their dream. When they called me to a meeting, I was only part prepared for the news.

"Yeah, business hasn't been good," Patrick admitted, although he didn't go as far as telling me he'd topped up my wages. I wasn't about to mention it because my behavior was akin to snooping and revealed I didn't trust him. "Warren's convinced me we should head out and follow our dreams. But, we're a bit shy of what we need to buy into the gym we've been offered."

"I hope you're not upset about me stealing your man," Warren added, a smirk of superiority on his giant gob.

"He was never my man, Warren. I'm pleased that he's found someone who will give him what he wants. I wasn't ever able to do that." I couldn't imagine, however, Patrick sticking his cock in Warren's concrete butt.

"We've been offered a major gig. Big money. Really big money. I'm talking 10K each. Plus tips."

I thought he was joking. "I'm not having sex with a donkey." They didn't laugh. "You're serious."

"Yeah."

"This doesn't involve surrendering my ass, does it?"

"You and your precious ass," Warren sneered. "What is it with straight guys and their ass?"

"What's the catch?" I asked.

"It's a gay bachelor party."

"Okay," I said. "So what changes from the usual set-up we do?"

"We ditch the sex toys. These guys have everything we sell, and more. This will be more down and dirty sex. You'll have to fuck ass, and I'll need to take real cock this time not some silicone wannabe attached to a chick."

"What's the climax of the night?"

"A dp."

I had to know. "Who gets double dipped?"

"Yet to be confirmed," Patrick said. "Either one of the grooms."

"I assume I'd be one part of the dp and Warren would be the other?"

"That's the thinking."

"I've done dp on a chick before. I never thought a guy could get two cocks in his ass. But, if you say so."

"Are you in?"

"Let it be understood. I don't suck and I don't rim and I don't get fucked."

"Understood."

We shook on it. I left Patrick's place wondering where my life would turn next. A house in the burbs with a hot wife and three kids. It might have once, but I think my dreams got bigger. I'd been agitated lately, probably picking up on the vibes that Patrick and Warren were on the verge of chucking it in. It wasn't as much fun for me either any more.

The town was boring me. Time for me to move on as well. I'd been told by enough people I had the face and the body and the charisma for movies. I'm vain enough that I believed them. I'd done a few amateur theatricals at college. I enjoyed the attention. I enjoyed the pussy it got me. Now it would get me boy pussy as well as the female variety. Hollywood? Yeah, why not? I had enough cash in the bank to keep me going for at least a year. If something didn't come up for me within six months though, I'd be outa there and try something else. I was young enough that I had time to make up my mind.

A gay buck's night. How bad could it be?

The ten grand appearance fee (plus tips) should have been an indication that it was going to be rough. Whether you think they got their money's worth and I was paid sufficiently for my time and trouble you'll have to decide.

The three of us went over a number of scenarios so we were prepared for just about any eventuality on the night. We knew from experience you couldn't anticipate everything that was bound to happen, but we knew each other well enough to adapt to any situation. I felt no apprehension when the big day arrived.

We took extra care with our preparation because it was gay and we suspected the partygoers would be more particular about personal hygiene. I'd given in on the rimming front. I'd agreed to allow dudes to lick my ass. Why not? I love it. Just as long as they didn't get carried away.

I needn't have worried as the house itself where the buck's night was to be held was respectability itself. I call it a house; it was actually a mansion and it purred wealth. This, then, was no down and dirty bachelor party. This reeked of elegance and good taste. I guess you can't judge a book by its cover.

Warren and Patrick drove over together and I followed later. I didn't want to be crushed to death between the two of them in Patrick's tiny van. Besides, I wanted an escape vehicle if things turned nasty. In the end I didn't need it but I wasn't to know that at the beginning of the evening when I rang the bell. The man who answered the door was in his early forties, very distinguished looking, and dressed casually in what I twigged were expensive designer clothes. There was nothing ostentatious about him. He had a fine ass as I noticed when he led me inside. "You must be Sammy. I'm Leonard, your host, but call me Len. Len, never Leo. Your two companions are already here. If there's anything you'd like to drink just ask one of the young waiters. Yes, they're available but we'd rather you saved yourself for the big event."

I didn't think I'd have any trouble getting it up. It was already hard from staring at Len's ass, so unless the rest of the guests were ugly as gargoyles my natural proclivities (as they were now) and the three cock stiffeners I'd taken earlier at Patrick's insistence should do the trick.

"I'd introduce you to the guests but your presence is a surprise, so I've put you and your friends into one of the guest rooms until the entertainment is due to begin. Please don't feel it's a slight."

I smiled. "I don't."

"Here we are." He opened a door to what would not have looked out of place in a European palace. It was an extravagant sitting room, probably much smaller than one in an overseas mansion but spectacular none the less. The furniture seemed to be genuine antique and in the best possible taste. A luxurious spread of food was set out and Warren was dispensing alcohol. Warren and Patrick looked right at home. "We should be ready for you in a little over half an hour. Make yourself comfortable." Len closed the door behind him.

"This is the life, Sammy," Patrick called. "I could get used to this."

"Name your poison," Warren said from the drinks cart which seemed to contain every high end alcoholic beverage known to humanity.

I don't usually drink before the entertainment but in this case I had a few butterflies making whoopee in my stomach. Not sure what brought on the nerves as I knew my cock was stiff enough that it was painful, so I'd have no trouble performing. I guess it was because I'd never been in a large group of gay men before. I didn't know what to expect. I assumed they'd be similar to a bunch of rowdy straight frat boys with female strippers in the room. That, on its own, was a terrifying thought. Now I knew how women felt.

The bourbon and coke helped more than I expected. I mellowed out, and had a second. I nibbled a little food wondering if Len did doggie bags for takeaway as it all looked so appetizing. Not a good idea before a performance though. That didn't seem to faze Warren and Patrick who gorged themselves as if they knew of a famine just around the corner.

It was boring sitting around waiting so we got onto the discussion of our futures. I was surprised to learn they were out of there in the morning. They'd already sold up most of their furniture and belongings and were heading west, driving in Patrick's van. As soon as they received their money for the night, they were off. I did wonder if they intended stiffing me and escaping with my share of the payment but Patrick, acutely aware of how their plans sounded, assured me that Len would pay us all individually.

Len knocked on the door about forty minutes later to tell us it was time. He led us along a corridor obviously used in days of old by the menial staff. It came out at a point overlooking the buck's night activities below. The men, about a dozen in number, were all naked, lounging about on divans and large cushions while watching a porn movie on the largest wide screen I had ever seen.

"The blond boy on the red divan stroking the man with the enormous pectorals. That's the groom you're to entertain."

The young man who can't have been more than a year or so older than me was beautiful. He had long blond hair that emphasized his effeminacy although his body was tight and muscular. He had a largish cock and when he stood to get himself another drink, his butt was perfection itself. "And that gentleman who just handed him a drink is his husband-to-be." His intended was equally as handsome but a good ten to fifteen years his senior. "Follow me, gentlemen, and I'll introduce you to the crowd."

We waited behind a curtain, Len's voice muffled by the huge crimson drapes that hid us from view. "What are we supposed to do?" I asked, suddenly aware that we had little prepared.

"Just gyrate around the room, let the guests tear your clothes off, until we arrive at Karl, the groom. Then we bugger the ass off him."

"All three of us at once?"

"No, the dp is the finale of the night. We'll let you know when it's about to happen."

"Sounds simple enough," I said, much too cocky for the way I felt.

Len finished his introduction and the drapes parted to catcalls and whistles. We were on. The lights were dim but bright enough to see our way amongst the guests, the porn movie casting ambient light as well although the sound had been somewhat muted so that it was now merely background grunts and expletives. It added immeasurably to the decadent feel of the bacchanalia. Karl, the blond twink, clapped his hands with delight when he saw us. He'd be a pleasure to fuck, so my rigid cock informed me. In fact,

I'd do him all night if I had the opportunity. Fuck, I'd do the entire room as long as my cock held out.

Fuck. I'd only had two drinks but it was like I'd had an entire bottle on an empty stomach. Those mongrel cunts. Warren had put something in my drink. I should have known. I'd murder the bastards. Trouble is…I didn't care. I felt so good, I wanted to make love to the entire human race.

My body automatically swayed to the rhythm of the music pumping through the room. I felt I was pulsating with life, like I was as one with humanity. I had wings on my ankles and I was an angel dispensing goodness to all the people at the party. They caressed my body, ripping off my constricting clothing as I passed, until I was naked, so they turned their attention to my nipples which they tortured with their nails and their teeth like a pack of hungry wolves. They squeezed my cock until it oozed juice, and fingered my balls until I thought they'd burst. Fingers prized open my butt cheeks before dipping into my moist hole until I swatted them away. I wasn't that far gone.

My journey had been slowed down by all the attention. I discovered Warren had already reached our quarry and was fucking Karl into submission. The young man was squealing for more until Patrick shut his mouth with his extra-large cock. Karl's boyfriend stood watching proudly, stroking Patrick's ass. As I swayed about the room watching the activity a number of men clamped their mouths over my prick to suck me dry but I had a task to fulfill and I didn't want my balls drained before I had a chance to sink my cock into Karl's hot insides.

Warren pounded him so heavily I thought there'd be little enough of Karl left to share, but the twink's screamed demands to 'fuck me harder' put paid to any idea he was fragile. Warren bellowed his climax as he shot his load into Karl's snug little hole, the mammoth muscle god dwarfing the twink's body. He slammed his groin against the pert little butt to get the last vestiges of spunk inside before he pulled out slowly, Karl's ass gaping, the spunk pooling just inside as Patrick took up position. Warren wiped his cock on Karl's face before the twink licked him clean.

The idea of sticking my cock in Karl's cum-filled ass was not exactly a turn-on. Sloppy seconds, or in this case sloppy thirds, was not my favorite position. I must have screwed my face up in disgust because within a few seconds a young waiter turned up at my side offering me a drink. "Len said it will make you feel better," he said. "Drink it all down at once."

It sounded like a command and my sluggish brain snapped to attention. I took the drink and skolled it. It burned nicely as it went down, rekindling the fire in my belly and my cock. So what if I usually went first at a gangbang, this was a gay party, things were done differently here. As the liquid fire spread throughout my body I was keen to take my turn. I wanted to fuck Karl to within an inch of his life, make him beg me to blow my load inside him.

I heard Patrick scream his orgasm before hands began to manhandle me forward. "How are you feeling?" Len asked, his enormous limp cock skidding across my thigh. Nice, I thought. I wonder what that would be like up my ass. I shook my head. Not going there. Concentrate on Karl's sweet hole. It was vacant now, Patrick having withdrawn. It was leaking, the spunk dribbling down his ass crack. Karl beckoned to me. "Come on and fuck me, Sammy. I want your cock."

Was there ever a nicer invitation? If so, I'd never received it. I moved forward, hypnotized by that sweet entrance, my cock eager to slip inside. I knew he'd been well and truly opened up so when I positioned the head of my prick in the slime oozing out of him, all I had to do was push and I slid in easily, surprised by how much grip his ass cunt muscles still possessed. My cock drove into a cavern of warm spunk and the feeling brought me close to losing my load. I thought of razor blades and rickety bridges to stop myself from coming although my cock was hard for the duration, the pills made sure of that.

I was flying again. I twisted Karl's nipples until I thought I'd rip them off but still he encouraged me to greater effort. I slammed his ass until it squelched like gum boots on a rainy afternoon, milking his prodigious cock in time with my thrusts. "Kiss me," he whispered hoarsely. It wasn't something I usually did, a little bit too gay to my mind, but ten grand can do a lot to persuade a guy. I leaned down to poke my tongue between his lips and he sucked me in with such a voracious force I thought he was sucking my soul out.

I stabbed his mouth with my tongue over and over until he whimpered under the combined onslaught of my tongue and my cock. I was invincible. The divan moved across the carpeted floor as I plowed his ass harder than I'd ever fucked anyone else before. I was possessed. All my concentration was in my cock and I wanted to come badly. I heard Karl's grunts and felt a warm wet splash between our bodies as his ass cunt muscles squeezed my prick. That was all it took. I screamed, slamming my cock so hard into his ass, adding to the accumulated slime, I thought he'd drown. I pumped what felt like gallons inside him until I fell prostrate on his body until I could recover my breath.

Karl stroked my hair and then whispered. "I want you to clean me out."

My stomach revolted. I attempted to get away but I was hemmed in by a number of men including Karl's betrothed who said, "If you do this, there's another drink for you after to wash the taste away."

As I was forced down onto my knees, Karl lay back on the divan, his butt hanging over the edge, his legs spread wide. His ass looked so inviting, so moist, so damn fucked. If I didn't think about the loads that Warren and Patrick had dumped inside, I could do this. Karl's ass was a cunt, I loved eating cunt. I banished the extra thoughts that made what I was about to do so unappealing. I concentrated and poked my tongue out, tasting male spunk for the first time ever.

At least it was my own – at first. It was slimy and warm. It didn't taste good, but it wasn't disgusting either. I licked again. I could get used it, I told myself.

"Come on, fag. Stop licking, eat it."

Rough hands pushed my mouth against Karl's ass. "Open up," someone commanded.

My brain had been short-wired by the booze to obey commands. I opened my mouth and sucked at Karl's luscious asshole. I'd heard about people who took their rimming fetish to extremes and now I was about to join their ranks. It seemed natural somehow. My mind, under the influence of whatever hypnotic Warren had slipped in my drink on Len's orders, made a sideways lurch and persuaded me there was little difference between sucking Traci's cunt and doing the same to Karl's. When you put it that way…

I took to my task eagerly, filling my mouth with the slime that had fermented in Karl's guts, swallowing it like it was choice zabaglione, admiring the taste and the texture.

"Oh my God," I heard Patrick exclaim. "He's fuckin' swallowing it all. Yeah, dude."

It must have taken five minutes or more but I gnawed at that hole until I got every bit of man juice sucked into my own stomach. Then I gave his hole one last appreciative kiss, licked my lips for any residual spunk, and sat on my heels in satisfaction.

Patrick held a large tumbler of bourbon out to me. "Here, it'll get rid of the taste."

I didn't really mind the taste but it seemed churlish to refuse a drink from a friend. It took three gulps to get the drink down and the heat burst in my brain like an explosive device. I rocked on my knees, expecting to find my head in pieces on the floor. "Wow, that stuff is good," I said. "It sure shakes out the cobwebs."

Some men helped me to my feet but I was too wobbly to stand on my own. I was grateful when Warren and Patrick came to my aid. "Enjoying yourself, buddy?" Warren asked.

"Having a great time," I replied.

Patrick smiled. "Well, it's about to get even better. How about letting Karl rim your ass as a reward for what you just did for him?"

I thought that sounded good and said so. Karl was a pretty fucker. "Here, let's get you in a comfortable position," Warren said. He and Patrick lay me on a padded device like you see in a chiropractor's surgery so that it could be lowered up and down according to what height you wanted. The difference was that there were stirrups for my knees so whoever knelt behind me had easy access to my butt without me putting any strain on my legs. I lay forward and waited for the exquisite feeling of a tongue against my hole.

Karl didn't disappoint. His tongue was as agile as his asshole and I was soon squirming in pleasure grinding my ass back for more. "You're a glutton for punishment," Karl said, standing up. The bench was adjusted and I felt something cold drizzle down my ass crack. I felt a finger breach my sphincter and started to struggle but it soon felt so good the hands that held me down were not needed. I backed up against the finger hoping whoever it was would push in another and tickle my prostate. He must have read my mind because a few seconds later his fingers brushed that small bud inside my anus making me jump.

It felt so good I hadn't noticed my face was now at crotch height and Patrick was stroking his cock near my mouth. I knew what he was after but I shook my head. "I don't do that."

"Just like you don't get fucked, eh?" he smirked.

Shit. He'd distracted me because now I felt a cock pressed against my ass. Before I could say no, I was breached. His knob was inside me. It felt like I'd been fucked by an elephant. I half turned to see Karl standing over me, his cock firmly wedged inside me. "Don't fight it, Sammy. You'll enjoy it more." He gave me about twenty seconds to get used to the feeling and then he slid in a few more inches, then a few more, until I felt him against my butt cheeks.

"You like that, don't you? Big macho jock who likes nothing better than hard cock in his ass. Busting his jock cherry. I've got my cock right up in your guts, fag boy."

I was about to demand he not call me that, when I felt a cock at my lips. I closed my teeth to bar the way but he pinched my nose until I opened up to breathe and he poked right in. It was Warren. He whispered what dire consequences there would be if I clamped my teeth down on his cock. He held my face and slammed into me, choking me until I couldn't breathe. He pulled out and repeated the exercise until I was ready to beg for mercy. He let me set the pace after that and I did my best to please him although I heard a sharp intake of breath from time to time when I hadn't shielded my teeth well enough.

Karl was pounding at my ass but by that time I was beginning to enjoy it, especially as he was very verbal in his appreciation of my cherry ass. As the grog seeped through my body, relaxing me even more, I knew I could fight and end up battered and bruised or I could lie back and enjoy it. The choice was easy. Mainly because it felt so good. I'd be sore in the morning, but I'd be ten grand richer. Plus tips. If I behaved myself, I hoped the tips would be greater.

Karl blew his load, filling my ass with ball batter, before Warren pulled out of my mouth to take his place behind me. He was a huge bastard and it hurt like hell at first. I got used to it, just as I got used to Patrick's, even taking his abuse about how he'd finally got to ride my ass after all the times I'd turned him down. Fuck, if I'd known it felt this good I might have given in earlier.

I think each and every one of the party guests took a turn at my throat and a turn at my ass. Some of the twink waiters joined in as well. All I know is that some hours later I was a mess of spunk, my ass twinged and I thought my jaw was dislocated. Some guys, Warren and Patrick amongst them, had returned for seconds, but I didn't care.

I welcomed the attention, begging them to use me. I didn't even care when I noticed guys filming me on their cell phones. There'd be repercussions but I'd be long gone.

I thought it was all over but then I was lifted in the air. Realizing what was about to happen, I struggled valiantly to get out of their grip. I saw Patrick lying on the floor, his cock aimed in the air as I was lowered on top of it. I barely felt him as he breached my sphincter, pulling my head down to tell me in no uncertain terms that I was merely a fuck toy for everyone at the party and that my ass belonged to anyone who wanted it from now on. A finger squeezed in beside Patrick's shaft, stretching me wider. Then two fingers until I thought my sphincter would snap.

Three fingers. I was in agony, the friction incredible. I relaxed momentarily when the fingers were removed, flinching in expectation of what was to come. I felt Warren's monster prick push at my ring. It burned like wildfire, opening me up slowly until the head was inside. I gasped for breath, Warren holding me firmly as he slipped another inch along his boyfriend's shaft, and I begged for mercy. Perspiration dampened my forehead and I shivered in pain but Warren kept pushing until with a groan of triumph he declared he was all the way inside.

They let me be for a few moments and I took great gulps of air to clear my head and ease the discomfort. I was just about prepared when they both began their thrust. At first, it was awkward co-ordinating their movements and I thought Warren's dick would fall out.

All things get better with time and soon enough, although it seemed like hours while I was in pain, I was getting high on having my ass stretched so wide. The entire party began to call me names, spitting at me, bombarding me with visions of what they wanted to do to my ass. Instead of turning me off, it had the opposite effect and I was high on cock. I begged to be impaled harder on their dicks and they obliged until I thought I'd faint with the sheer ornery pleasure of what they were doing.

Just as I was learning to appreciate their pricks thrusting into me, Patrick let loose in my bowels, followed quickly by Warren. As my innards were flooded, I tugged my own cock to its final orgasm of the night. After they pulled out, leaving my hole gaping and sore, I collapsed in a heap.

By the time everyone had finished with me, the sun was coming up. Len helped me up. "I guess you'd like a shower?"

"Sounds good."

"How about I run a bath and you can soak in it."

"Sounds even better."

About fifteen minutes later I slid into the hot water leavened with some sort of scented salts that smelled of relaxation and contentment.

"I'll come and get you when breakfast is ready," Len said.

"Warren and Patrick?"

"They left hours ago. Headed off on their little adventure to LA."

The euphoria of the previous night had worn off, but apart from a few muscle cramps and aches and pains I felt none the worse for wear, although my ass gaped so wide I thought my liver and my kidneys would fall out. I guess I felt humiliated being used like a whore, but that's what I was. Had been ever since I'd pimped my body at the first hen's night. It didn't matter, it was just a word. It was just a way to make a living.

Len came back to help me out of the bath because I was so relaxed my bones felt like they were made of jelly. He wrapped me in a luxurious terry-toweling robe, guiding me out onto the terrace where I was offered toast, coffee, bacon, eggs, pancakes, sausages, enough to feed an army. "You trying to get me fat?" I laughed as I tucked in. I was ravenous. "What next? Fatten up the jock, baste him in sperm and serve him up at dinner with a nice mint sauce and Chianti?"

Len laughed. "That's something we've never tried." He looked at me suspiciously. "No regrets? No abuse? No threats to go to the police? No nothing at all?"

"Would it do me any good?" I asked between mouthfuls.

"Nope."

"Then why waste my energy complaining?"

"Look," Len said seriously. "I didn't know it was a revenge thing by Warren and Patrick otherwise I wouldn't have countenanced what went on."

"Okay," I replied.

"You're a nice kid. And the fee for last night and the tips, well, you made yourself a bundle. I know it's none of my business, but I'd get out of this town as fast as my car could take me."

"Duly noted and already planned."

"Good. But what's in the future for Sammy?"

I shrugged.

"You seem like a pretty pragmatic guy. It's none of my business but I like the way you handle yourself and I know a man who might have a job for you." My ears pricked up at that. "I sent him the footage of you in action last night. I know, I should have asked your permission first but considering how many partygoers were taking movies you'll be all over the net by now."

"I've given up being a whore, so if he's…"

"Nothing like that. He's a producer/director in Hollywood."

"Don't think my body's made for porn."

"Not porn. Not in the Spielberg class either. More your exploitation pic director using the untalented relatives of major stars for the Asian market. You ever thought of being an actor?"

"Funny you should ask that…"

Yeah, fate is a funny bastard. This Hollywood dude, Lyle Pritchard, turned out to be legit. Fuck me.

I packed up and headed west. It would take a couple of days to reach the Hollywood Hills where Pritchard lived. I actually enjoyed myself on the way to my future. If

Pritchard didn't pan out there'd be other opportunities and time enough to plan my revenge against the two bastards who inadvertently gave me more pleasure than they knew, as well as opening up innumerable opportunities. Turns out I enjoy sex anywhere/any time. I know because on my road trip I was fucked by a trucker in the men's room of a sleazy roadside diner. I compensated a day later by boning a plump waitress in a storage room while her husband flipped burgers out front. I enjoyed both experiences more than I can say.

Pritchard lived in a house even more palatial than Len's although it had none of the taste. A bit like Lyle himself. He was into conspicuous consumption and bought all his friends and acquaintances with a shovelful of coke for each as well as unlimited booze and sex. When I buzzed the front gate for admission saying just "I'm Sammy Jackson. Len said you were expecting me," Lyle replied, "Come on in, son, and join the party."

When I was introduced to the semi-naked crowd of men and women around the pool with a view of Hollywood Boulevard, I knew my reaction that afternoon was a test, an audition. Didn't matter. I was primed and ready for anything. I fucked cunt, I fucked ass, and I fucked throats both male and female. I had cocks in my butt. I played the game. Pritchard himself was a man with no morals that I've ever discovered. But he was a man with versatile tastes, a huge cock, and an insatiable appetite for cock, cunt and ass, belonging to men and women around my age. He was easy on the eye and his mansion had all the mod cons: drugs, sex, babes, boys, all laid on like the power and the water supply. And he really did put me in his movies. I moved in with him. His house was big enough we could go for days without running into each other.

As for my acting? Let's just say, I'll never win an Oscar, but I've got a cult following amongst those with less pretentious tastes than the critics. My movies bring in a steady income and sell well on DVD. I usually have my shirt off through most of the movie and flash my ass on a regular basis. My cock also features from time to time and has its own fan club. Gay boys have begun discovering my…um…assets and Lyle has an idea for a bisexual action hero franchise starring yours truly. He's promised I'll get to choose my leading man and he's even contemplated a hardcore version for when I get older. Retirement package, he calls it. I think he's just a sleaze. But I love the guy in my own twisted way.

Oh, before I sign off. Yeah, I found Warren and Patrick. I landed on my feet so I didn't feel too bad about what they did. They were on the last of their money when I tracked down their miserable gym. I couldn't help myself. I turned their business around with carefully planted stories that I liked to work out there because of the privacy and the fact they allowed me to do it close to naked. Muscle queens are so predictable – they flocked there. So shoot me, I don't hold grudges.

What did I get in exchange? A life of luxury, a cushy job, more sex than I know what to do with, and fame. You can't go wrong with fame. I'm stashing my money aside for a rainy day. I know this lifestyle won't last forever. I may be a jock, but I ain't dumb.

WANNA SHARE YOUR HUSBAND?

Randy's ass was a work of art. It was round, plump but muscular, smooth as a billiard ball, a tight puckered hole, and as supple as bamboo in the wind. Not that we could see any of those attributes right now because it was clad in tight fitting cut-off jeans which showed how snug it was without revealing the full extent of its delights. It helped that the ass in question belonged to one hot dude, at that moment stripped to the waist, his olive skin drawn over firm muscles gleamed with the perspiration that cascaded off his body as he helped a group of workmen manhandle a large sheet of plasterboard into place.

We were on a building construction site and if the reaction of the group of men I was showing around was anything to go by, Randy himself was the building's major sight. It didn't hurt sales that he was showing enough crack when he bent over that the entire party threatened to drown in appreciative drool.

"Throw that in with each apartment and you've got me sold," Ethan Temple, the pretentious outspoken alpha of the group, slobbered.

"What an ass," Ralph agreed. "I could fuck that all night."

"You think he's gay?" Alec asked.

Ralph ostentatiously adjusted his crotch making no secret of his attraction. "If only."

At that moment, Randy looked up and, seeing the group, waved, his face lit up by one of his incredible transforming smiles.

Temple groaned. "That mouth was born to suck cock. My cock."

I looked at the men's fitted trousers and noticed distinct stirrings in the loin departments. These guys were openly turned on by one of the construction workers and weren't afraid to show it. After a few words with his work mates, Randy made his way through the jungle of pipes, tools, and construction material toward us.

Alec hissed. "OMG! He's coming over. Be still my pulsating cock."

"I hope he's not a top," Ralph panted.

Ethan's response was succinct. "Who cares? You just flip him over and fuck him. Any guy with an ass that hot should get ploughed on a regular basis."

You may wonder why I would put up with guys talking about another man like this. Okay, I guess we've all been guilty of similar braggadocio in the privacy of our own home, but these guys were here in an official capacity; looking at buying real estate. They were seriously wealthy and seriously interested in buying into the complex in which we were standing. Grevillea Gardens was slated to become a modern luxury oasis on the edge of the central business district, smack bang in the middle of the gay area of town. The developers knew their market.

They'd wanted someone with an 'in' to the said market to promote the over-priced condominiums. I'd suggested a few of the local gay papers and magazines, and after the chairman of the board had overcome his distaste for everything faggoty, I was the PR bunny shanghaied to show prospective buyers around. That list, consisting of people who had emailed for one of our highly colored and highly artistically enhanced brochures extolling the virtues of 'community' living (my euphemism), was a veritable Who's Who of the moneyed gay class.

I'd watched the complex grow from a motley collection of old Victorian shop fronts that had been scarred by generational upgrading until they bore little resemblance to their original design, so ugly and battered it was only humane they were put out of their misery, through a monstrous gaping hole in the ground which would become the three-level underground car park, to the concrete and glass structure that was taking shape before our very eyes. It was going to be a magnificent addition to the city; for those who could afford it. Just as Randy was a magnificent addition to the eye candy of the same city.

"Randy," I greeted the worker as he approached. (a few of them snickered at his name) "I'd like you to meet a few of the men who are interested in…um…" I was being deliberately provocative but if the men in the group heard me they didn't care because they swarmed on him like starving locusts, introducing themselves by praising his muscles (asking for a feel), and his construction prowess, even though I doubt any of these guys could tell the difference between a hammer and a screwdriver. Temple showed his admiration by going so far as to squeeze his ass when he thought no one was looking.

I, however, watched their every move, barely suppressing my jealousy.

When he finally managed to extricate himself from the sticky-fingered gay Hydra, I couldn't help myself. "Randy, these guys are wondering if you come with the purchase price of each apartment."

So wealthy and prominent in all the right Establishment circles were they, my comments didn't even embarrass them. Money and power, it seems, papered over crass and predatory behavior.

Randy laughed. "Flattering as it is, guys, I'm not for sale."

Temple sneered. "Every man has his price."

That was such a cliché. And Temple was such a jerk. But a prestigious one.

"Besides," Randy added, before pulling me forward by the lapels of my suit until he could paste his mouth over mine in a tonsils-deep kiss that threatened to detonate my dick, "I'm already spoken for. And I'm a one-man man."

At this point, they really should have looked embarrassed, given what they'd been saying about Randy earlier. Not a bit of it. In fact, now they'd discovered he was gay, it was like feeding time at the zoo.

Temple rose above the hubbub. "You and…uh…"

"Jake Chalmers," I prompted, but he ignored me.

"You must come over for one of my soirées." I hated that Temple managed to pack so many meanings into the last sentence, including one that had every sordid back-alley encounter one could imagine oozing from each syllable. I wasn't the only one to notice because his friends all babbled their agreement, their heads bobbing enthusiastically like the bobble-headed dogs people keep on the dashboard of their car.

Randy put his arm around my waist while leaving enough space between us that his sweaty body didn't stain my suit. "As long as the invite is for the both of us," he answered.

Temple turned his fakest smile on me, "Of course, I wouldn't have it any other way."

I didn't like the snarky way he said it. Call me jealous, but my trouble-ometer was working overtime. Still, I had to keep these guys on side, the sales success of Grevillea Gardens depended on it. With this group of men investing in the complex, success was assured. Thwart them and I could kiss goodbye to my career. I gritted my teeth. "We'd be delighted."

Randy let go of me. "I gotta get back to work. See you guys later. Pleasure meeting you Ethan…" He rattled off everyone's name as he looked them in the eye. They were impressed. But then, Randy was a very impressive piece of work.

I noticed him the first time I visited the construction site at the behest of the architect, Ted Pace, who wanted me in from the beginning. At that stage the building was little more than a concrete shell. His enthusiasm for the project was infectious and I could picture his dream in my mind as he described the apartments in great detail, right down to the imported fittings and the color schemes. I must admit to a certain envy even though there was no way I could ever afford to live in the building. The quarterly body corporate fees alone would cripple me.

"Who's the worker in the cut-offs?" I enquired as casually as possible.

Ted knew I was gay and his eyes wrinkled in amusement. "Fancy him, do you?"

My response was to blush.

"Hey, Randy," Ted called. "Over here."

I had time to study the young man as he made his way over to where we were standing examining Ted's floor plans. He was breathtakingly gorgeous. Nicely muscled, great legs, even greater chest and arms, and a face that could launch a thousand wet dreams. What made him even more delicious was he wore heavy workmen's boots with thick woolen socks rolled down. Yum.

"What's up, Ted?" he asked.

"I'd like you to meet, Jake Chalmers."

I held out my hand and the moment his skin touched mine I almost pulled back at the electric shock that surged through my arm.

"Wow," Randy smirked. "Did you feel that? Instant electricity."

Ted was even more embarrassing. "I knew you two would get on. Just as well as you'll be seeing a lot of each other."

"So, tell me. Why will we be seeing more of each other?" Randy's open smile drew me like a moth hypnotized by a candle.

"Jake here is the PR guy for the entire project."

Randy whistled in admiration. At least, that's what it sounded like.

"His CV is probably higher than this building. He's one of the top in his field," Ted continued.

"No shit," Randy said, appraising me in a new light. Was he impressed, or was he interested? I couldn't tell. All I knew was that I was definitely interested. I just hoped it didn't show.

"He'll be taking journalists and politicians and other big wigs around as the building takes shape. Then prospective buyers. Men with the sort of money that keeps us both employed. They'll be paying a large fortune for these condos, so if they want a little extra luxury here, or a change in color there, perhaps it would be a good idea to bend over backwards to help.

Randy smiled sweetly. "As most of these apartments are aimed at wealthy gay men, don't you mean just plain bend over?"

I didn't detect any overt hostility to gay men so I guessed he was making a joke.

Ted cleared his throat. "Um…Jake here is gay."

Randy looked stricken.

"But I'm not wealthy," I added quickly to put him at his ease.

"Sorry. I'm always making stupid remarks that get me into trouble."

"I didn't take offense."

"Thanks. Look, I better get back to work, otherwise the guys will think I'm bludging."

I was sorry to see him go. We didn't do the usual social niceties. You know, the 'pleased to meet you' routine. He walked away whistling.

Ted laughed. "He likes you."

"What do you mean?"

"The tent in his shorts more than matched the one in your trousers."

I was mortified, quickly tucking myself down, hoping Randy hadn't noticed. Then it struck me. "Randy's gay?"

"As gay as you are," Ted replied. "And, before you ask, even though I don't know if such things matter to you, he's not seeing anyone at the moment. And I know you're not, so…" He shrugged.

"Regular little matchmaker, aren't you?"

"All part of the service," Ted joked.

I took more notice of Randy over the following days. He always had a shy smile whenever he looked up and caught me staring. Occasionally he would adjust his very ample crotch as if to tease. There was something about him that appealed to me, apart from the obvious eye candy qualities he possessed. We were both coy with each other even as I attempted to pluck up the courage to invite him out; but we never seemed to get a moment alone.

Until the day I got a complaint about him.

Normally I would have taken a note of the dissatisfaction and filed it in my bin after the complainant had left but Ziggy Kowalski was much too important a man to dismiss lightly.

"He was downright rude and abusive. Doesn't know his place. I want him fired," he demanded, his face fiery red from his temper.

It took me a good half hour to calm him down and persuade him that I would be able to handle the situation to his satisfaction, offering that Randy would be dismissed if the accusation was true.

"What do you mean 'if'?" Kowalski raged. "Are you doubting my word, because if you are—"

I'd was sick of this belligerent fool but he had enough sway in the business community to not only have my job but bring the whole project to its knees. "Of course, I'm not doubting your word, Mr. Kowalski," I said quickly. "But there are processes which have to be followed. We have to work within the legal system here otherwise there will be repercussions not only against the project but against your own companies. The union is very strong in the building industry and does not tolerate its members being treated in a cavalier manner. If I'm not mistaken, your company has a contract out for a resort on the north coast…"

I left the sentence unfinished so the full import of what I'd said had time to sink in.

"Do it your way, but the outcome had better be what I want."

He stormed out of my office. It was my fault Randy was in this jam. Kowalski had arrived at a very inopportune time insisting he wanted to see the view from the highest level. He was about to marry his long-term fiancée and believed the penthouse was ideal. He knew it was purported to be a gay-friendly complex which should have been hint enough that it was not exactly conducive to the needs of a straight stud like Kowalski whose temper was as legendary as his good looks. He'd knocked the teeth out of more than one paparazzo in his time as well as bashing a presumptuous gay admirer whose common sense had been over-ruled by his cock.

Money changed hands on each occasion and the press soon tired of pursuing the litigious billionaire.

The rumor mill among the cognoscenti had it that Kowalski was Sugar Daddy to the latest twink television soap star and that the penthouse was to be his reward for keeping his mouth shut and his ass open. Even knowing so little about Randy I couldn't see the behavior that Kowalski had described to me as being in his nature – unless he was provoked.

I called him in. "Take a seat, Randy."

"This is about Kowalski, right?"

I nodded.

"Am I fired?"

"I don't have the authority to fire you—"

"All it would take is a word from you."

I was trying to remain upbeat. "Tell me what happened."

"The guy squeezed my ass. When I told him it was inappropriate he just laughed and said 'I'm Ziggy Kowalski, I can touch who I like.' I told him in no uncertain terms that he couldn't touch me. He tried it again. Tried to shove his hand down the back of my shorts. I wrenched his arm back up behind his back and told him if he touched me again I'd break his fuckin' arm in so many places he wouldn't be able to wank for a month."

Despite the seriousness of the situation, I laughed.

"You believe me?" he asked.

"Of course, I believe you," I said. "He accused you of offering yourself in exchange for cash. When he turned you down you supposedly disrespected him."

"I better pack my tools away then."

"Not yet. You trust me?"

"Yeah."

I picked up the phone and dialed the number on the card Kowalski had left. After a brief explanation to his personal secretary I was put through.

"I've been expecting your call. Have you fired the bastard?" he bellowed.

"Afraid it's become a little more serious than that. The worker has contacted the union and he's counter-charged a lot of serious shit…" I let him get the string of four-letter words out of his system before continuing. "I've arranged a meeting for tomorrow. I think we can sort this out to everyone's satisfaction."

He consulted his diary and we agreed on three o'clock the next afternoon.

Kowalski couldn't leave well enough alone. "I'll see the bastard rot in hell. He doesn't know who he's dealing with here."

He slammed the phone down so hard my ears were still ringing when I turned to Randy. I was about to explain the gist of the conversation when he said, "I heard every word. Loud bastard, isn't he?"

"Can you bring a union rep with you but tell him to zip it until I've had my say. I don't want him to bugger up what I have in mind."

"I'll bring Phil; he knows when to keep mum and when to charge in like a bull at a gate."

Randy got up to leave but turned before he reached the door. "Thanks. I appreciate what you're trying to do, and no matter how it turns out, I'm grateful you were on my side."

I wanted to invite him out for a drink but I thought it may have given him the wrong idea. He hesitated at the door but then mumbled his thanks again and disappeared back to his job.

The next day I had my desk and five chairs set up for the confrontation. If my little plan didn't work it was just as likely I'd be looking for a new job as well. As expected, Kowalski turned up with a lawyer which is why I'd asked Randy to bring a union rep. Kowalski looked surprised by the number of chairs until Randy and Phil arrived a few minutes later. "Who's this?" the billionaire demanded.

"Union rep," Randy said.

Kowalski glared at me, noticing for the first time the videotape I had on my desk. He blanched momentarily but the composure was back in place seconds later.

"There seems to have been some unfortunate miscommunication yesterday between Mr. Kowalski and Mr. Simpson," I explained.

I noticed Kowalski wince when I placed the Mr. in front of Randy's name, implying an equality in status he would never acknowledge. "There was no miscommunication, the bastard was…" Kowalski blustered until his lawyer put a hand on his arm to calm him down.

"If both parties will allow, I'll put their sides of the story as succinctly and unemotionally as possible. Please don't interrupt. If I leave anything out you will both get an opportunity to add anything I've missed. Is that agreeable?"

Randy and his rep agreed easily, Kowalski only after huffing and puffing and whispered consultation with his legal representative.

True to my word I gave both sides, Kowalski turning beetroot as I outlined Randy's accusations. I thought he would explode, his face was so purple. All the while I turned the video around and around in my hands as if it was a nervous habit, ensuring that the handwritten label was often in his direction. Kowalski glanced at it from time to time. It took a while but eventually he must have been able to see the words clearly because he stiffened momentarily. What he would have seen was Security video Level 26, and yesterday's date.

In conclusion, I said, "I suspect this has all been a case of mistaken interpretation and I think an apology from both sides and a handshake should settle the matter once and for all."

Kowalski's lawyer spoke. "Are you suggesting Mr. Kowalski is not telling the truth? That you're taking the word of a…a common worker over one of the richest men in the country. Are you seriously suggesting my client is a predatory fag?"

I bristled, finding it difficult not to put this homophobic pipsqueak in his place by suggesting honesty had very little to do with wealth, but I held my tongue. "I'm suggesting no such thing," I said with an edge to my voice. "But if Mr. Kowalski insists on pursuing this matter then I will be obliged to hand yesterday's security tape of the incident to the police for their decision on whose truth is the more valid."

"Would you give us a moment, please," the lawyer asked as Kowalski tugged at his arm.

Randy, Phil and I left the office, walking far enough away that we could not hear the conversation although the body language on both Kowalski and his lawyer was anything but amicable. Much head-shaking from the lawyer and eyes cast toward my desk where I had left the video was followed by Kowalski's explosive temper and arm waving. Finally, when it all subsided, we were called back to my office.

The lawyer did all the speaking. "Mr. Kowalski has always been the worker's friend and would never knowingly put a young man out on the streets by depriving him of his job."

I bit the inside of my cheek to stop myself from guffawing at such a blatant lie. How Randy and Phil kept their cool, I have no idea.

He continued. "Mr. Kowalski is prepared to accept Mr. Simpson's apology and let things be."

I could see Randy's union rep about to rise to the bait so I got in quickly. "I think the deal was that both sides offer an apology in good faith without either side admitting fault."

"I don't think my client is prepared to be that forgiving."

We could all play this bluff game. I scooped the security video off my desk, stood up and pointed to the door.

"Thanks you, gentlemen, for coming this afternoon. I'm sorry we couldn't reach an amicable settlement."

"Now, hold on," Kowalski interrupted. "If you let me have the video I'm sure we can bring all this unpleasantness to a close."

"I wish I could oblige you, Mr. Kowalski," I lied. "But for legal reasons I have to hold on to this tape for a certain period of time. Health and Safety, and all that shit. After that, you have my guarantee that it will disappear forever. You need have no fear of its sudden appearance anywhere. Your lawyer is your witness."

Another bout of whispering and Kowalski sighed. "Very well." He extended his hand in a rather miserly fashion to Randy who took it and pumped it energetically.

"I'm sorry if there was any misunderstanding," Randy said.

"Me, too." Kowalski mumbled. It was a less-than-fulsome apology but it was the best we would get.

After a little small talk Kowalski and his lawyer left the building and the three of us remaining sat down. I poured us all stiff drinks.

"I think you let him off rather easily," Phil complained.

"I wouldn't say that," I replied, stress perspiration soaking under my arms.

"Oh?"

I picked up the video and peeled off the sticker that read Security to reveal the label underneath. It was *The Sound of Music*. "There is no security camera on level 26."

Phil was surprised. "It was all a bluff?"

I nodded.

"Well, fuck me," Phil exclaimed. He held out his hand to shake mine. "Well played. I hope you'll always be on our side, Mr. Chalmers."

"When your side is in the right," I replied.

"I'd best get back," Phil said, swallowing the last of the liquor. "You coming, Randy?"

"I'd like to speak to Jake for a few minutes, if that's all right with both of you," I said.

"Not a problem," Phil said, grabbing his hard hat and heading across the building.

Randy and I watched until he disappeared from view. Before I'd even had a chance to smile at Randy, he was in my lap, his lips pasted to mine, his tongue pressing into my mouth until I relaxed and put my arms around him.

When we'd surfaced for air, all I could say was, "Wow."

"I've wanted to do that since the first day I saw you," he admitted.

"So that was not a gratitude kiss?"

"Nah, that was a 'let's-stop-wasting-time-and-get-it-on' kiss. Not that I'm ungrateful. In fact, I'll show you just how grateful I am." He wiggled his ass against my super-hard cock as a preview of what was to come.

"You want to do it here, right now? Or can you possibly wait until after I take you out to dinner tonight?"

He laughed. "Under the circumstances I think fuck first, date second. How's that sound?"

"Perfect."

And it was. Randy was perfect in every way: he was smart, funny, gorgeous, a firecracker in bed, an insatiable bottom (my favorite kind), loving, and so into me it made my eyes mist. Sure we dated – after the event – but that was a formality; mainly to see if the perfect night we'd spent making love was a once only bells-ringing experience. I guessed if the subsequent couplings didn't almost equal, or exceed, the initial sexual explosion, then a relationship was not meant to be.

One of things that immediately attracted me to Randy, apart from his obvious physical attributes, was his desire for a stable relationship. He was ambitious in that regard to an almost alarming degree. On our first dinner date, he exposed the full extent of his dreams for the future. If mine hadn't so closely meshed with his, I think I might have laughed at the sheer impossibility of what he envisaged for the future. Good friends, good food, good times, and just one good man to make it all worthwhile. I liked that he was into monogamy.

We were on our second date when he revealed the impossible, both a little high from another bout of extraordinary love-making and, I admit, a goodly portion of expensive wine imbibed with dinner. We sort of dared each other in what could have been a folly, but…

We decided to make out on the building site where we both worked. We knew Bert, the security guy. We also knew that he had a phobia about heights so once we checked in, he wouldn't be following us to the rooftop. Sure, he was surprised to see us late at night but he loaned us one of his spare flashlights and we wended our way carefully through the building detritus and machinery. We almost changed our minds as we climbed the concrete stairs to the upper floors. I have no idea how long it took, what between our constant stopping to exchange kisses, our chasing each other a few flights until we lay exhausted among the dirt and cement dust, and our euphoria that we had found in each other our almost perfect partner.

Once we reached the top floor, the feeling was exhilarating. We held hands as we approached the edge of the building, the lights of the city and the harbor set out before us like randomly thrown, twinkling confetti. We watched the ferries ply their passengers across the harbor beneath the eerie, illuminated high span of the grey metal bridge.

"What I wouldn't give to live here," Randy sighed. It was part of his impossible dream.

"Me, too." I replied. My dream was equally ambitious and as far out of reach as Randy's. We couldn't even afford a deposit on the front step, let alone the penthouse.

We made unhurried love on the dusty concrete floor as we watched the city go about its business twenty-six floors below, blissfully unaware of our activity. Afterwards Bert bid us goodnight, ignoring the dusty and disheveled state of our clothing and the no doubt smug satisfaction on our faces. Everything about our futures was uncertain except that we would be together. We couldn't marry as such – not yet anyway – but that night we trothed our love with the exchange of rings as we sent our wishes fluttering out into the universe.

After the weekend, we came back down to earth. Ted approached me Monday morning with the news. "Kowalski has withdrawn his offer on the penthouse. Told the papers it wasn't up to his standard and that he'd only just discovered it was a building aimed at faggots."

I admit I'd half expected it. "Right, so we immediately go into damage control."

Ted noticed the ring on my finger. "Oh, my God. You and Randy did it, didn't you?" His face beamed his satisfaction. "You sly fuckers. I knew you'd be good for each other." He hugged me, heartily slapping me on the back.

"We intended telling you but we only decided on the weekend," I said. I explained about our tryst in the shell of the future penthouse.

Ted elbowed me. "You romantic bastard."

"Am I going to have the company on my back because of Kowalski pulling out?"

"Put it this way, they're less than pleased and your balls were on the line but then Kowalski went and saved your gonads with his homophobic slurs.

I could breathe easy for the moment. "Thanks, Ted, for bringing me up to speed."

He was about to leave when he stopped and, taking a deep breath, said, "Mate, my brother was gay. I just wish he'd had people like you and Randy looking after his back."

I noticed his eyes mist briefly. He sniffed once and was back to his usual self. I let my questions go. "Thanks, Ted. I owe you."

"Nah, just invite me to the wedding."

Once I was alone in my office, I set my mind to thinking about how to salvage the hot-water-deep-shit situation in which I found myself. I'm not top of my PR field for nothing and by mid-morning I was so engrossed in retrieving victory from defeat that I was taking no calls and fobbing off VIP visitors to Ted. He understood, just as he understood I'd make it up to him some day. Kowalski's comments had been reported locally so I ensured, by means of social media, that they went viral, trending as the day went on. It was picked up by the local gay press who owed Kowalski no favors although the mainstream media were somewhat tardier in exposing the story. Eventually, it went international, mainly because of Kowalski's reputation as one of the richest men in the world. Not Bill Gates wealthy, but enough to make a number of prestigious lists, so he was news, especially when the gay community called for a boycott of his company. Kowalski held out until even he realized he was on a one-way beating to nowhere. Then, via his lawyer, he issued a half-hearted retraction that accused his enemies of taking his words out of context, even though there was video of him saying the exact same words he now disowned.

That was part one of my strategy. I would have to wait overnight to see if the second part panned out. Randy and I spent a restless night together, wondering whether my future job prospects were in jeopardy. It was early morning before I finally fell asleep after continually getting up from bed to check my computer for any updates on the situation. I had deliberately avoided any contact with my PR firm bosses until my scheme had reached fruition. So I was grumpy as a Disney dwarf by the time the smell of coffee woke me from a deep abbreviated sleep.

I wandered into the kitchen of my apartment, scratching my balls in a most undignified manner.

"You should let me do that," Randy joked, as he poured me a large heart-starter.

"If I let you do that," I yawned, "I'd never get to the office."

"You want breakfast?"

"Just this coffee is fine. Bit too keyed up to eat."

Randy had been at his laptop on the kitchen bench and turned it in my direction. "Speaking of which…"

I glanced at the screen and my appetite returned.

"Maybe I could go some toast and scrambled eggs."

"I thought you might."

As Randy prepared breakfast I scrolled through the news and finance stories on the net. Kowalski's company's shares had dropped in the late afternoon the day before, nothing precipitous but enough for him to issue a more fulsome apology for his disparaging remarks albeit complaining about political correctness run amuck and bemoaning the death of free speech. It must have been even more galling for him to open his financial newspapers that morning to discover that he had unintentionally lifted the profile of Grevillea Gardens more than the hundreds of thousands of dollars poured into PR so far.

In fact, the developers were receiving enquiries about buying into the complex from as far away as Europe, Asia and the Americas. I smiled in satisfaction as I closed the computer and tucked into Randy's delicious scrambled eggs. I looked at my watch; there would be just enough time for a celebratory fuck and a shower (maybe both together) before we left for work.

The PR Company was left in no doubt the increased profile of Grevillea Gardens was as a direct result of my intervention. They in turn big-noted themselves to the developer. The thanks trickled back to me as did the promise of a bonus at the end of the year if I kept up the momentum. It's a fine line between extravagant praise and a summary dismissal.

Randy and I found more and more depth to our relationship as we fell even more hopelessly in love, always promising each other that we'd one day have it all including the penthouse in Grevillea Gardens or another complex like it. It was a pipe dream but it was fun just the same. I would have done anything for Randy and I knew he would do anything to make me happy.

He also got astute at warding off unwanted attention from predatory gay guys who came to inspect the building as it took shape. I was kept busy with the VIPs and even Ted pitched in from time to time when the congestion of the just plain inquisitive became a bottleneck. The penthouse, however, remained a problem. That is, until I hit upon the idea of featuring the workers on the site in provocative poses accompanied by a little biographical information. Some of the guys baulked at the idea – there were no women on the site, construction work being one of the last bastions of sexism – but the majority of them joined in the fun even though they were straight. The website became so popular that we were inundated with requests for big color posters of some of the guys, especially Randy who had a fan club in a matter of hours after his photo and biog appeared. It seemed not to matter a jot that he listed his status as 'Monogamous relationship.' That seemed to spur people on to greater efforts to win him over. All with a singular lack of success.

Enter Ethan Temple, more wealth than most mere mortals possess and impeccable taste to go with it. Not in the stratospheric levels that Kowalski claimed but enough to pay off the national debt of most small countries. He was an arbiter of gay chic, followed by social climbers and the old moneyed alike. They clamored for his opinion given freely via his website, his television program on antiques, and his newspaper column. If his readers and viewers got the advice for free, his publishers paid through the nose for the privilege of sending his words out into the world.

He was a charismatic man, handsome as the devil, and with that same creature's morals. When his PA rang to schedule an appointment to look over the building, especially the penthouse, I made every obsequious effort short of kissing his ass to sway him in the building's favor. Even if he didn't buy, a favorable mention on one of his programs or in his column guaranteed another avalanche of enquiries.

After Temple and his group took their leave, whispering like a gaggle of hens all the while perving on the workers, especially Randy, I thought the complex would be on the receiving end of a right bollocking. I probably could have played it smoother but Temple got on my wick. I needn't have worried because nothing appeared or was said by the Gay Guru that week or the next.

The week after that I received another phone call from Temple's PA, informing me that his highfalutin-ness was interested in doing a spread on the Grevillea complex in his next newspaper column. I almost choked. "If the developers could see their way to taking out a teeny advertisement somewhere in the newspaper, I'm sure the coverage would be favorable," the male PA purred down the phone, his mellifluous tones emphasizing the veiled threat that if the developers didn't take out the requisite advert then coverage of the building would be less favorable.

I Informed the PA that I didn't foresee a problem, neglecting to mention my loathing of advertorial to which many newspapers have stooped in a futile attempt to stave off bankruptcy. Just before he hung up, he mentioned, "Do have that lovely tradesman you featured on the website last week make himself available as Mr. Temple is bringing a photographer." Again, there was no mistaking the PA's innuendo.

There was also no mistaking that I was not wanted when Temple and his new entourage descended on the building. I was relegated to the sidelines while Randy was poked and prodded and then whisked behind a modesty screen while an assistant kept my attention focused on giving the boring details of Grevillea Gardens' history. I wasn't concerned for Randy, he could take care of himself, so I smiled when I heard the all-too-familiar sounds of someone being slapped in the face followed by Randy admonition, "Keep your hands above my waist or else I'll walk and you can get someone else to take my place."

"Don't be like that, honey," I heard Temple say. "We're here to make you a star."

Randy sounded unimpressed. "I thought you were here to promote yourself and maybe Grevillea Gardens."

"Play your cards right and your profile may just end up bigger than this apartment building."

"If I'm *nice* to you, is that it?"

"Depends on how nice," Temple snickered.

"Not gonna happen," Randy snapped.

Temple seemed unfazed. "Everybody has their price."

It seemed to take forever for the shots of Randy to be taken and he was careful at all times not to be photographed in the altogether no matter how hard the photographer attempted to catch him unawares and no matter how hard the production crew were getting, not least of all Ethan Temple himself. It was all too obvious.

I was surprised that Temple was so effusive in his praise when the article appeared a few days later under the banner headline across two pages: Are These the New Gay Faces of Sydney? The two faces in question were the artist's impression of Grevillea Gardens, and Randy's. Plus there was a half-page of Randy with his delectable ass covered by little more than his tool belt.

Did that bring the punters in!

Ethan Temple, of course, believed we owed him an enormous favor because the apartments were being snapped up. As well, he put down a hefty deposit for the penthouse. Suddenly, Randy became his new Best Friend as did I by default, courtesy of being Randy's partner though there was damn little courtesy shown me when I was with him. Randy lapped up the attention, wallowing in his new-found notoriety. He even picked up a number of modeling gigs and got an agent. Nice money toward our future, of course, but Temple began to hog his time and attention in order to rub his face in the luxuries of life that would be his by jumping relationships. However, he remained steadfast.

Temple ensured the penthouse was completed first. He wanted the honor of being number one. The lower floor apartments were almost complete, merely in need of some finishing touches, the elevators were working, the complex a matter of weeks away from the official unveiling. He got permission to throw the Party of the Year to which the city's glitterati turned out. Our invitation was addressed to Randy Simpson and Companion. I had been thoroughly sidelined.

Randy, insulted on my behalf at the invitational slight, was happy to stay home – we were sharing my apartment at that stage – but I knew how much he wanted to see Temple's design flair for himself. He was concerned that I would be snubbed and that he would be propositioned by various men at the party. It wasn't vanity, Randy's body had become a negotiable asset thanks to Ethan Temple's promotion. Neither of us was comfortable about it. If our love hadn't been as strong as it was, I would have been worried. I persuaded him we should attend. "I'm a big boy, I can look after myself," I joked.

As it was, the evening passed memorably. Temple made no attempt to monopolize Randy's attention, nor did he belittle me further than saying, "Oh, you're still together, I thought you would have split up ages ago." I laughed it off but I could see Randy was gritting his teeth. I didn't mind my boyfriend being in the spotlight. People whispered as he entered a room, pointing him out as someone of importance. Men and women forced business and personal cards on him attempting to solicit a call-back.

The furnishings and fabrics that Temple had chosen were, to use an old-fashioned word, exquisite. Not my style, too ornate, but it was all designed in the best possible taste. "It looks like a showroom," Randy commented, and I had to agree. The view was what made it magic and the partygoers congregated on the vast deck that circumnavigated the building.

"What do you think?" Temple was mellow by this time from the copious amounts of alcohol we had watched him consume.

"Beautiful," Randy exclaimed.

I just managed, "Extraordinary." Temple took it as a compliment.

"How would you like to live here?" Temple asked.

"It would be a dream come true," Randy admitted.

"If you play your cards right, some dreams really do come true."

After dropping that carrot and stick, Temple turned on his heels and went to speak to other people across the large living area off the deck.

"Is he serious?" Randy asked.

I wasn't sure.

"It's tempting," Randy laughed.

I must have turned pale, because he hugged me quickly, assuring me he was only joking. It was the sort of joke that ripped my heart out. "I think it's time we left."

"Yeah," Randy agreed, casting one last longing look around the spectacular view. "No use pining for what you can't have."

"Wait here, I'll get our coats."

I went searching down the corridors for someone who knew where our coats were, becoming increasingly disoriented in the maze of corridors, only to be bailed up by Temple's PA who thrust a large glass of very strong liquor into my hand insisting I drink it all up because it was the most expensive alcohol I was ever likely to taste. He bored me rigid for a good twenty minutes before he let me go, taking the dregs of my drink with him. Now, more than our coats, I needed to find a toilet. I needed to piss badly.

Opening the first door I came across, I discovered it was a bedroom, with a walk-in wardrobe larger than some inner-city cottages. The bathroom was next to the closet and I ducked in to relieve myself. After I'd completed my business, I splashed cold water on my rather ravaged face and was about to go in search of our coats when I heard the bedroom door open. I assumed it was another guest looking for his or her coat too until I recognized Randy's voice, I was sure of it. I was about to call out to alert him to my whereabouts when his voice became giggly and furtive. There was someone with him; someone who sounded very much like Ethan Temple. A third voice, I didn't recognize.

Extinguishing the light, I opened the bathroom door and, being new, it made not a sound. I crept to the edge of the walk-in closet and peered around the corner into the vast expanse of the bedroom. If I was caught I would merely say I'd been looking for our coats and that would be that.

Temple was cutting white powder on the glass topped table in the center of the room.

"I don't think Jake would like it if he caught me taking drugs."

Damn Right!

Randy told me he never touched them yet he was glancing longingly as Temple formed three lines.

"How will he ever find out, Randy?" Temple said, putting his arm around my boyfriend's shoulder in a much too familiar manner. "He's gone home and left you here. We couldn't find him anywhere."

"Yeah," Randy said, sounding unconvinced.

Suddenly, I began to feel woozy. I'm no genius when it comes to maths but it didn't take me long to put the requisite addition together. They must have thought that if they drugged my drink, the one Temple's PA so adamantly insisted I consume, it would leave Randy at their mercy. Ordinarily, I would have said they were dreaming, but with Randy's head full of booze and the lure of wealth and luxury, perhaps they stood a slight chance.

Temple snorted the second line, leaving just one remaining.

The third member of the group whom I now recognized as Ralph, nudged Randy. "Go on, you'll like it."

"And you'll give a better performance. You'll be more relaxed," Temple added.

Randy was still reluctant. "I don't know. What if Jake finds out?"

"How's he gonna do that? We aren't going to tell him."

"I know. If he finds out, I'll tell him you tricked me," Randy said, delighted with his lie.

"Yeah, that'll work," Ralph said sarcastically. Randy couldn't see him and Temple cast their eyes heavenward because he was too busy leaning over the line of coke hoovering it into his nose. Randy sniffed when he'd finished, rubbing the back of his hand against his nostrils. "How long does this shit take to work?"

"You'll be buzzing by the time you do your strip… um…dance."

Randy looked concerned. "You're sure Jake's gone home because if he catches me…"

"Just concentrate on the money the guys are gonna put in your undies," Ralph said, his patience wearing thin. "Come on; let's get this show on the road."

"Your costume's on the bed. I'll give you ten minutes to get changed then I'll come and fetch you and give you the big introduction. The guys will only be putting fifties in your briefs," Temple smirked, rubbing his hand across Randy's butt cheeks. Randy didn't remove it.

"And there'll be no touching?"

"Not for fifty lousy bucks."

Temple went to the door. "Ten minutes."

Whatever they'd put in my drink had finally made its way through my system and as Randy changed in preparation for his dance, a show I should have put a stop to immediately, my head went sort of numb and I blacked out. I had no idea how long I was unconscious but I came to in the same position so no one had found me. My head pounded and I was still groggy. I heard loud music from outside and the sounds of men cheering and whooping it up.

Attempting to pull myself up by one of the coats hanging in the closet, all I managed was to dislodge a whole rail of wooden hangers. I was pelted in the head and had to put my arms over myself for protection. When the cascade subsided, I managed to get on my hands and knees to crawl across the floor to the bed, using it to lever myself into a standing position. I was wobbly on my feet so I used the wall to steady myself as I stumbled out of the bedroom and into the long hallway, heading toward the throbbing sound of music.

The end of the corridor opened out into the living area where a number of men were congregating gazing through the open glass sun deck doors at the activity around the pool. A young guy, woo-hooing his lungs out saw me and reached out to steady me. "Man, what are you on?" he asked.

"Wish I knew," I replied.

"Gotta get me some of that. You're so fuckin' wasted."

"Tell me about it."

"You missed most of the show."

"What show?"

The kid snickered. "That construction guy that's so popular. He's selling lap dances. Starting stripping for fifties then the guys upped the ante if he'd do a lap dance."

"You join in?"

"Too rich for my wallet," he said, looking disappointed.

"Mine, too," I commiserated.

I watched closely as Randy sashayed his body around the pool, straddling anyone who put a hundred dollar note in his briefs or his socks which were already bulging with cash. Temple had his back turned to the action, speaking on his mobile phone. I wondered what he was up to. The main party must have broken up while I was out cold because there were no more than twenty-five men – no women – in attendance now. Those with the cash were pawing Randy's ass as he wiggled and strutted, pulling the back of his briefs down to reveal he had no tan line. There was a definite feel of rabid testosterone in the air. I was amazed Randy had managed to keep his briefs on. Despite calls for him to take them off, he resisted.

The music stopped suddenly. Temple addressed the crowd. "Seems our little Randy is shy. I once heard his boyfriend say that Randy couldn't be bought, isn't that right, Randy?"

Randy had a goofy grin on his face. "That's right."

"Whereas," Temple continued, "I believe every man has his price, including young Randy here."

The audience yahooed.

"Not me," Randy called over the excessive noise.

"How about we test it, to see who's right," Temple suggested. "You game, Randy?"

"Hell, yeah," he said.

"Okay, let's open the bidding."

Randy giggled, "I hope you're not taking an auctioneer's fee."

"No. Every cent of it goes to you."

Randy had already extracted the notes from his socks and undies and a considerable wad it was, too. He kissed it, I suspect for good luck.

"You want me to hold those notes for you?" Temple asked,

Randy shook his head. "Uh huh. My mum told me there were only two places for cash. In your pocket or in your hand. As I ain't got no pockets, I'll keep it right here where I can see it."

The audience roared its approval at his gauche home-spun philosophy. This was an entirely new side to my boyfriend I'd never seen before.

"What am I bid for Randy to show us his delectable ass?"

Randy turned around as if on cue and Temple ran his hand over his cheeks, a little too lovingly for my liking. "Come on, guys."

A fat old queen lounging in a sun chair, yelled, "A hundred bucks."

Randy shook his head.

"No deal," Temple cried.

This went on for a short while until the bidding got to five hundred and Randy shouted, "Deal."

Randy went to collect his money and the guy his prize. The two of them disappeared into a bedroom for about three or four minutes before they returned, Randy with his cash and the winner giving the thumbs up.

"How about his cock, guys?" Temple asked, fondling the front of Randy's briefs until his cock hardened, almost breaching the waistband, leaving a sticky patch near the outline of the head. The audience groaned at the sheer size of his weapon.

"Randy's a top, guys. I have it on good authority that what he has between his legs is a whopper. Take a look for yourselves."

A member of the audience yelled out he was willing to part with three hundred dollars for the privilege of unveiling Randy's family jewels. The bidding quickly got to a grand at which point Randy cried, "Sold," and he disappeared again into the side bedroom to claim the cash. I thought he'd sold himself cheap.

My head was beginning to clear but my body simply wouldn't follow my commands. It was as if there was a disconnect between my brain and my limbs. I remained propped up against the wall. When Randy returned triumphantly, his winner moved his hands apart to signify the length of Randy's dick. It was no exaggeration and I could see a few people regretted they hadn't bid higher.

"So far, Randy has been pretty easy. Most men will show off what they have on offer, but can Randy really be bought and sold like some commodity."

Randy shook his head vehemently while the audience cheered and shouted "Yes."

"Let's try it then shall we?"

A cheer went up.

"First, let's take a short break because Randy must be exhausted after his dance routine and the strenuous lap dances. What's say we let him freshen up and you guys can get yourselves a new drink."

The guy standing next to me offered to get me a soda and I took him up on the offer, hoping that he hadn't recognized me and wasn't in on the drug fuck. He came back with a Coke and a little blue tablet. "They're giving them out at the bar. Suggesting we should all take one or two. I got you one." Handing out cock stiffeners did not auger well.

I saw Temple and Ralph heading toward the bedroom with Randy. I ducked along the passageway ahead of them and went back to my hiding place hoping they wouldn't see me. When they came in, Randy was bopping around on the souls of his feet.

"How you feelin', Randy?" Ralph asked.

"I sure am." Randy snickered at his own joke.

"How about another snort? Make you feel real euphoric. You'll be on top of the world," Temple said.

"But I won't lose my moral compass, will I?" Randy asked.

Who was this man? He wasn't talking like any Randy I'd got up close and personal with.

"That's what we're testing, Randy," Temple said while Ralph crushed up crystals that looked suspiciously like ice rather than coke. They were really playing big time now.

While Temple kept Randy's attention focused, Ralph crushed the crystal meth into three lines and offered the first to Randy who noticed no difference to what he's snorted before. He extracted one of the hundred dollar notes from the pile in his hand and rolled it up, snorting the powder, rubbing the side of his nose when he'd finished. Temple was next, and then Ralph. By the time the three of them had done their line, Randy was raring to go.

Randy headed for the door. "Let's get this experiment under way. I can feel a rush coming on." He didn't see Temple and Ralph high five each other in triumph.

The living room had been transformed while we'd been in the bedroom. It was too cold and windy on the deck now so everyone had moved inside, armchairs arranged in a semi-circle around the large wooden coffee table which was set-up like a make-shift stage.

Temple called for quiet. I eased back into my former position, the young man having grabbed himself a more comfortable seat in the front row. Feeling parched, I chugged a fair guzzle of my soda, wiping my mouth with the back of my hand. "What am I bid on Randy's butt hole?" Temple asked.

The bidding was fast and furious. When the bid reached a staggering amount, Randy appeared conflicted for about ten seconds and then shouted, "Done."

"No more sneaking off to the bedroom for a private viewing any more. Randy, assume the position and show the lucky winner, and all of us here tonight, your cute little butthole."

Randy looked taken aback at this development. It didn't seem to be at all to his liking. But then, almost as if the meth wiped away his conscience, he kneeled on one of the scattered cushions on the coffee table, and pulled off his briefs.

"Show us, Randy."

Obedient to the last, he reached back and pulled his ass cheeks apart until his moist brown bud was obvious to all.

"Stay there, Randy. Who wants a feel?"

Just about every man in the room put his hand up.

"Let's say, fifty bucks to cop a feel, eh, Randy?"

"Sounds fair to me," he said.

He kneeled like a bitch on heat as the men in the room lined up to finger his ass, some sneaking a squeeze of his cock or balls as well, until he'd been extensively finger fucked, his hole slick with lube.

"Now, for the biggest test of all," Temple proclaimed. "Who wants to fuck Randy's cute, tight little hole?"

Randy turned around to object. "I don't do that. I'm a top."

Temple pushed his head down. "That will make it so much more interesting for the highest bidder."

"If I accept." Poor Randy still believed he had the power of veto.

Temple was all confidence. "Oh, you will, you will."

But Temple was wrong. No matter how high the bids climbed, Randy was adamant and turned them down. Eventually it got to ridiculous levels, but still he wouldn't give in. Just as the men at the party were becoming disenchanted, the door to the penthouse opened and in strode Kowalski, a brief case in his hand. "Am I too late?" he bellowed.

"Just in time," Temple said.

"What are we bidding on?" Kowalski asked.

"Randy's asshole. We're bidding to see if Randy will allow someone to fuck it. Says he's a top but we all know money turns us any which way if it's a high enough price."

"What was the last bid," Kowalski asked. He whistled when he was told. "And the slut didn't take it?"

I felt sick to the stomach now and decided it was time to stop the charade, but my mouth simply would work.

Kowalski looked around the room. "Where's the fucker's boyfriend?"

The young man who had brought me the drink pointed me out. "Over there."

So he was in on it. Bastard.

"Drag him over here to the front where he can see what a fuck-up his precious boyfriend is."

Hands grabbed me, lifting me bodily to carry me across the room and dump me unceremoniously near Randy. On seeing me, he appeared guilt-stricken and attempted to get up and cover himself. Temple grabbed him by the throat to hold him in place. "We're not finished, Randy. You can't leave until the auction's over. You're the guest of honor."

"Okay, let's not fuck around here," Kowalski said. Addressing me, he continued, "You reckon your boyfriend is unbuyable."

I couldn't speak, so I merely nodded.

"Bullshit," Kowalski spat. "I'll prove it to you." He extracted a great wad of cash from his coat pocket and waved it in Randy's face. "This is all yours if you bend over so I can fuck your ass, whether you're a bottom or not. What do you say?"

Randy's answer was succinct. "Fuck off."

Kowalski shrugged. He picked up his briefcase and clicked it open. "What about this?"

The communal gasp was shattering. I prayed Randy would turn it down. For a moment he looked at it. He picked up a bundle to ensure the notes were all of the same ridiculously high denomination and that there were no fakes embedded in the piles.

"It's all real, Randy. No fakes, no substitutions. I'm a man of honor."

I almost choked at that statement.

I could see Randy making mental calculations of exactly how much was in the briefcase. It was a small fortune.

Finally, he said, "Yeah, for that you can fuck me."

I sobbed, Kowalski triumphant at my expense. "Don't do it, Randy," I begged.

Temple patted me on the head like a pet animal. "There, there. Maybe when you're rich and famous you'll be able to buy and sell people just as readily."

Kowalski had already stripped off his clothes to reveal a portly body covered in dark hair, with enough musculature to show he worked out sufficiently at a gym so he wasn't soft. He thrust his semi-tumescent cock between Randy's lips. "Get me hard, boy. Once you feel my cock in that sweet ass of yours, you'll never want anyone else."

Randy opened up to suck Kowalski's thick cock. The partygoers leaned forward for a better view, a view that I was all-too-close to. I wanted to pluck out my eyes but I was held down by two of Temple's helpers.

"Mouth like velvet," Kowalski sighed, his cock expanding until Randy could barely stretch his lips around it. "Love to blow my load down your throat but it's your ass I paid for." Kowalski moved behind Randy, kneeled on one of the cushions and held him by the waist. Aiming his cock at Randy's lubed hole, Kowalski pushed. Randy screamed in pain, begging him to take it out but Kowalski smirked proudly. "How does it feel to be fucked by a real man, eh, boy? You like it. Maybe not now but once you relax, you're gonna love feeling my rich cock fucking your guts. I'm gonna breed your ass, ride you till you can't stand up."

I glanced about and noticed a number of men in the room had also removed their clothes and were stroking their cocks while watching the live porn show acted out in front of them.

Kowalski looked directly at me. "Look at him, dickwad. Does this look like a man who can't be bought? Groveling before my cock. Before the night is over, he'll be addicted to cock, everyone's cock, any cock that wants to fuck his ass. He'll be a slave to cock and there's no more powerful cock than mine, is there, Randy? Look in your boyfriend's eyes and tell him what you want."

Randy looked directly at me and although I could see part of it was the drugs talking, deep down I could see that this was what Randy wanted.

"Your cock is the best, sir. I want to worship your mighty cock with my ass. It's yours, sir. Use it any way you want."

"Any way I want, Randy. You sure?"

"Fuck, yeah. If I'm gonna be fucked in the ass, I want to be fucked by the top man and you're the top man, sir. My ass is your slut hole."

Randy had begun panting which was the signal the fuck was getting to him.

"That's it slut boy, squeeze those ass muscles around my cock. That's it. You want to please me?"

"Yes, sir. Anything you want, sir."

"Is that your boyfriend's wedding ring you've got on your finger?"

"Yes, sir."

"Take it off. Give it to me."

Without the slightest hesitation, Randy removed the ring and handed it back to the man slamming his ass. Kowalski pulled out. "Turn around, Randy."

My boyfriend shuffled around on his knees until his red puffy asshole was in my face. Kowalski fingered the wedding ring. "Cheap piece of shit, this is. I'm gonna put it where it deserves to be." With that, he pushed it against Randy's sphincter until it disappeared inside, Then he rammed his cock back inside as well. "That's what I think of it, boy. What do you think?"

"I think your cock is all I need, sir. It fills me up like nobody else ever has. I can feel your strength inside me, opening me wide."

"You know why I'm opening you up, boy?"

"No, sir."

"Because you're gonna entertain my mates here until the sun comes up. What do you think of that, slut?"

"I don't think I could do that, sir."

"Oh, I think you will. And you'll beg for more."

Kowalski nodded and Temple joined him. He had a syringe in his hand.

"How about a little booty bump?" Temple asked.

Kowalski pulled out momentarily so Temple could shove the needle-less syringe into Randy's ass, squirting the liquid meth deep inside, before plunging his cock back in. "Give him three minutes and he'll be begging to be gang fucked. Might be a bit abrasive on your cocks gentlemen but I can assure you we can turn this top fucker into a slut bottom before the sun rises, no doubt about it. He's a natural."

A cheer went up and the remaining men stripped out of their clothes to crowd around Randy. He'd lowered his head as the drug inside him began to take effect, his face revealing the euphoria he must have been feeling as the insatiable Randy took over.

To my horror, my cock was concrete hard as I watched Kowalski sweat over Randy's back.

Suddenly Randy roared as if he had been asleep too long and Kowalski's cock had suddenly awakened him like the prince's kiss on sleeping beauty.

"Kiss him, Randy, show him what a total fuck slut you are."

Randy hissed, "Yes, sir," and turned like some human cobra ready to strike. His cock was hard and leaking a huge amount of pre-cum, his face a twisted horror as his tongue flicked in and out. He grabbed the back of my head and sank his tongue inside me, biting my lip, drawing blood. His face was like some savage as he explored my mouth and I couldn't pull back, mesmerized by his power. I felt the thrusts as Kowalski entered him again and again. I was in agony but simultaneously so turned on I just wanted relief, although none was forthcoming. I was not permitted to touch my cock.

"That's enough. I want to watch you take care of my buddies now," Kowalski demanded.

Temple was first to shove his short stumpy prick into Randy's mouth. "Suck him, slut. Open your throat, that's right." I could hear Randy gag as Temple showed no mercy. "Not good enough for you once, now look who's got his cock in your throat. I bet you love it."

Temple held Randy's head and hate fucked his face, Randy's body moving with the sensual slither of a large prehistoric lizard, others jerking off over his body. One of them, too impatient to wait, shoved his cock into my mouth until he unloaded down my throat.

Kowalski bellowed, slam dunking his cock in Randy's hole until his animal grunts of ejaculation stopped and he fell exhausted on Randy's back. There was an expectant pause in the action as Kowalski pulled out, his cock dripping slime. He came over to me and wiped his limp prick against my lips until I opened up. "Lick it clean." I got my tongue under the head and into every cranny of his thick cock, sucking until the taste of his spunk was no more.

"Okay, guys," he said as he grabbed his clothes and began dressing. "He's all yours. Fuck him all night for all I care. His ass is perfect, all the better because he didn't want to give it up. So fuck him good and hard so he'll remember the night he became a cock slut and we bought his ass." He tapped the briefcase as he passed. "Worth every penny. Pity you didn't realize it's only pocket money to someone with my assets."

Once Kowalski left, Temple took charge. "I want you up here every afternoon, slut. On your back, legs in the air so the first thing I see when I come through the door is your ass. After I've shoved my cock inside you, you'll take care of any my friends who happen to stop by. And once they hear that Randy the Construction Worker's ass is on tap 24/7, I think I can safely say my penthouse will be the go-to destination for anyone who likes tight working class butthole."

Temple rough fucked Randy, screaming a string of expletives that turned the air blue, my boyfriend sobbing his need for cock, begging to be fed hot spunk.

Over the next few hours everyone at the party obliged until his body was covered with slime, his face thick with cum porridge. The only person in the room who hadn't taken a turn was me.

Temple taunted me. "Look at him, Jake. You still want this cum whore? Show us what you think of your boyfriend now."

I wrenched my cock out of my jeans, my briefs soaked with pre-cum, aiming at Randy's sex-crazed face. "You fuckin' sleazy cum pig." I spat in his face, the gob landing in his open mouth as he slithered about the floor like a giant human dragon, spunk spilling from his ass as he slipped across the floor, trying to find cock, believing it was his only salvation.

He sat between my legs finally, his mouth agape, begging for my load. I was happy to add my spooge to the streaks and slime trails all over his face. His tongue darted out to taste the drops that fell into his mouth. My boyfriend had been transformed from a loving man into a crazed sex monster.

I didn't have time to think about it as Temple instructed his minions to get rid of us. Randy had the presence of mind to grab his underwear in which he'd stored the loose cash from his dancing, and I grabbed the briefcase. The front door to the penthouse was slammed behind us.

We both hung our heads in shame as we headed to the elevator, unable to look at each other on the journey down, although Randy began to giggle. I slapped him on the arm which set him off even more. We didn't want the sound to travel up the lift shaft in case anyone heard.

We stopped off at my office. I didn't have the luxury of a shower but I did have a toilet with a washbasin. Randy cleaned up as best he could, expelling the slime from his ass until his wedding ring emerged. I placed it back on his finger, kissing him passionately. "I love you," he whispered. "It happened exactly as you predicted."

"That's the secret of good PR," I said. "Create a market for something that's impossible to buy and then watch people trip over one another to pay through the teeth for it. It's just basic supply and demand. And I think after tonight you can probably afford to raise your prices. But a new campaign is in order."

"You should take up acting," Randy said.

"I'm not half as good as you are. Those screams almost had me convinced you really were a top even though I know you're one of the best bottoms in the business."

We both laughed.

"I needed that shit they pumped into me though," he said. "Otherwise I don't think I could have taken that many cocks."

"Did you enjoy it?"

"Don't hate me, but yeah."

"I don't hate you. You did it for us. I'm glad you got pleasure out of it. Just don't make it a habit behind my back."

"No way," he pledged. "I'm a one-man man."

Grevillea Gardens was completed on time and on budget. Randy and I moved into our third floor apartment in the complex courtesy of a briefcase full of cash and our combined savings. Randy's extremely popular with the neighbors, although he keeps them at arm's length. It adds to the mystique. He's had a few offers but the price is definitely not right. Yet.

I need to work on my covert PR campaign for him. After all, we have to pay for our dreams. Those building fees are a bugger.

Besides, we have our sights set on moving into the penthouse one day.

Lydian Press

ABOUT THE AUTHOR

Barry Lowe writes about love and sex so he won't forget how to do it. When he's not out doing field research, he's writing about love's wonderful variations for a series of smut eBooks, novels and anthologies for Lydian Press

Go to www.barrylowe.info

OTHER WORKS BY BARRY LOWE

Available in eBook and Print

PLAYS

THE DEATH OF PETER PAN: Gay Historical Romance

NOVELS & ANTHOLOGIES

BUSTING BILLY'S BUTT: A Gay Erotic Romance

Steve and Billy's monogamous relationship has gone stale until Billy, ever the exhibitionist, shows them a way to spice up their sex life.

THE MAJOR AND THE MINERS: A Gay Historical Romance

1930s Australia: Two men from opposite ends of the social spectrum. Is love enough to overcome the obstacles between them?

THE GRAVY TRAIN: A Murder Mystery with Recipes

Someone on the train has an appetite for murder!

A TOUCH OF THE SON: A Gay Novel

Their secret passion will lead them to hell. Will they be able to find their way back?

ROMANCING THE BONE: Gay Romance Erotica

OMG! NOT ANOTHER GAY EROTICA ANTHOLOGY?

ROUGH & READY: Gay Tough Guy Erotica

YOUR BOYFRIEND IS HOT: Gay Cuckold Erotica

BEAR SKIN: Hot Gay Bear Erotica

THE MORE THE MERRIER: Gay Gangbang Erotica

THE BOY IS A BOTTOM: Gay Anal Erotica

COCK-EYED OPTIMISTS: Gay Romance Erotica

BABY, I'M NOT A MONSTER: Gay Vampire and Other Paranormal Erotica

CHRISTMAS CRACKER: Gay Erotica for the Holidays

BUTT BOYS: Gay Anal Erotica

HOW MUCH IS THAT DOGGIE IN THE WINDOW?

BACHELOR BOY

THE BI-WORD

EVERYTHING'S COMING UP ROSES

SELECTED SHORT FICTION

Available as eBooks

LOVE WITH A SIDE ORDER OF PELICANS

CHRISTMAS IN JULY

BREEDING MY BOYFRIEND

NEW JOCK IN TOWN

BACHELOR BOY

SUMMER AT RAINBOW COVE

I WAS A MALE NYMPHO FOR THE FBI

HOW MUCH IS THAT DOGGIE IN THE WINDOW?

THE DAY OF THE CLIFFORDS

HE WON'T SEND ROSES

A RED ROSE BEFORE CRYING

PRIDE AND JOY

ROAD HUMP

THE GOOD, THE BAD, AND THE CUDDLY

THE GROOM CLOSET

TUNNEL VISION

HARD ON HIS HEELS

SPIN THE BOTTOM

THE NEW DAD'S CLUB

FOUR ON THE FLOOR

TAGGED BY THE TEAM

WANNA SHARE YOUR HUSBAND

For all Barry's titles please visit his page at: lydianpress.com

Lydian Press is dedicated to bringing you the
finest GLBTQ erotic literature on the web.

Visit us on the web at:

http://lydianpress.com

www.ingramcontent.com/pod-product-compliance
Lightning Source LLC
Chambersburg PA
CBHW051057050726
47592CB00002B/567